THE
NOH
MASK
MURDER

PRAISE FOR *THE TATTOO MURDER*

'A tale that fizzes with intrigue and ingenuity'

DAILY MAIL

'Like voyeurs, we follow Takagi down the charred streets of bombed-out Tokyo to scenes of fastidiously executed decadence'

THE NEW YORK TIMES

'This lurid mystery provides a fascinating portrait of wartorn Tokyo'

THE TIMES CRIME CLUB, PICK OF THE WEEK

'Intricate, fantastic and utterly absorbing'

KIRKUS REVIEWS

'Crackles with the energy that made Takagi one of Japan's most popular crime authors'

FINANCIAL TIMES

'The extensive and nuanced portrayal of Japanese subcultures makes *The Tattoo Murder* an absorbing and satisfying read'

BUSINESS POST

'A delightful, different book, not only because of its unusual setting and premise, but because Takagi is a powerful plotter and constructor of fascinating, complex characters'

THE A.V. CLUB

AKIMITSU TAKAGI was born in Japan in 1920 and went on to work as an aeronautical engineer until the end of the Second World War. He later decided to become a mystery writer on the recommendation of a fortune teller. He went on to become one of the country's most popular crime authors, winning the prestigious Mystery Writers Club Award for *The Noh Mask Murder*. Takagi's debut novel, *The Tattoo Murder*, is also available from Pushkin Vertigo.

JESSE KIRKWOOD is a literary translator working from Japanese into English. The recipient of the 2020 Harvill Secker Young Translators' Prize, his translations include *The Kamogawa Food Detectives* by Hisashi Kashiwai, *Tokyo Express* by Seicho Matsumoto and *A Perfect Day to Be Alone* by Nanae Aoyama.

THE NOH MASK MURDER

AKIMITSU TAKAGI

TRANSLATED FROM THE JAPANESE BY
JESSE KIRKWOOD

PUSHKIN VERTIGO

Pushkin Press
Somerset House, Strand
London WC2R 1LA

English translation rights arranged with The Heirs of
Akimitsu Takagi through The Sakai Agency

The Noh Mask Murder was first published in Japanese as *Nomen Satsujin Jiken* in 1949

First published by Pushkin Press in 2024

3 5 7 9 8 6 4 2

ISBN 13: 978-1-78227-965-5

Designed and typeset by Tetragon, London
Printed and bound in the United Kingdom by Clays Ltd, Elcograf S.p.A.

www.pushkinpress.com

THE NOH MASK MURDER

Prologue

In the summer of 1946, a year after the end of the war, at a bathing resort on the Miura peninsula in Kanagawa prefecture, I ran into an old school friend. His name was Koichi Yanagi.

He had only recently returned to Japan, having been deployed to Burma shortly after earning a chemistry degree. I, on the other hand, had been rejected from the army on the grounds of poor health and, after working as an engineer at a munitions company until the end of the war, now found myself staying at the Marine Hotel, which overlooked the resort in question.

Back then, the idea of writing a detective novel hadn't yet crossed my mind, but that didn't stop me from lugging around various classics of the genre—books I had devoured over and over since childhood, often to the detriment of my actual eating habits.

Of course, Koichi knew all about this passion of mine. During our schooldays, I hadn't been content simply to read what others had written, but would occasionally play the detective myself, poking my nose into some real-life mystery I was convinced required solving.

'You know, Akimitsu,' he once said to me, 'if you're so unhappy working as an engineer, why don't you start a detective agency? Or write your own mystery novel?'

I wasn't entirely sure he was joking.

'Of course I'd like to be a detective, but who's going to hire me? As for writing a novel, well, I've never attempted anything like that. If I *were* to give it a try, though, I've always thought

I'd like to write something a little different from your average whodunnit …'

'Something a little different?'

'See, most detective novels have some hapless Watson-type following Sherlock Holmes or whoever around and relaying his dazzling exploits to the reader. It's all a little dull, really. Then there are the ones where the detective himself turns out to be the criminal, but these days that's starting to feel rather stale too. There's even the idea of the Watson-style narrator confessing that he was the murderer all along, but Agatha Christie already did that quite masterfully with *The Murder of Roger Ackroyd* …'

'Well then, how would you write your novel?'

'I'd have the detective solving a genuine real-life mystery, and narrating his actions as he does so—a first-hand account, if you like. But it wouldn't be one of those pulpy, old-fashioned memoirs where the detective makes himself out to be a real hotshot. The focus would still be on logical reasoning, you see, but it would be much more than a simple record of the investigation. Instead of the detective merely stating what he did, on what date, with whom and so on, all that detailed evidence would form the basis for a meticulous account of his every thought, his precise chain of reasoning—and all the actions he took as a result.

'Of course, it'd be a very hard format to pull off. Firstly, you'd need an incredibly elaborate real-life crime to solve—it'd be no good relying on some half-baked or accidental murder for your mystery. Secondly, you'd need a whole range of attributes to write the thing: the physical stamina to traipse around gathering clues, the deductive skills to analyse them effectively, and then the literary talent to set it all down convincingly in writing. I do wonder if any one human could ever possess all three attributes in sufficient quantity …

'Still, I'd certainly like to give it a try one day. I'd tackle some fiendish real-life mystery, then set down precisely how I solved it in the form of a novel. My readers would be presented with the exact same evidence as the author. They'd be able to follow the detective-narrator's train of thought, assess the appropriateness of his actions—and even come up with their own alternatives. But I don't imagine an opportunity like that will ever present itself ...'

'Well, Akimitsu, if anyone ever comes looking for a detective, I'll know where to send them!'

This, at least, I assumed to be a joke. But it wasn't long until, making good on his promise, Koichi relayed to me a desperate plea for help from a man named Taijiro Chizui. Alarmed by the letter requesting my aid—and one enigmatic phrase in particular: *I finally learned who was behind the mask!*— we made our way to the Chizui mansion. But by then, it was too late.

My would-be client was found dead in an armchair in his bedroom. What was more, the room was completely sealed, and no wounds were visible on the body. If it hadn't been for that fearsome Noh mask, said to harbour a two-hundred-year-old curse, staring coldly into space from the floor, or the three coffins that someone had ordered from the undertaker in advance, we might well have concluded that he'd merely died from a heart attack.

But once the curtains had opened on this tragedy, the Chizui family was plunged into catastrophe after catastrophe—and at a terrifying speed. Three coffins turned out to be too few. Before long, the entire illustrious family had reached its demise.

Then there was that jasmine fragrance lingering around the corpses, not to mention the other 'props'—a spray of maple

9

leaves and a Noh costume with snake-scale patterning—that, along with the mask, suggested the advent of some evil spirit. In a sort a dramatic flourish, it even seemed as though the demon's magic powers had rendered the immutable laws of physics completely irrelevant.

Faced with a case like this, I was overcome by a kind of fervour. Hoping to make my long-cherished dream a reality, I tackled it with all the energy I could muster. But the result was—well, perhaps you can imagine. I was forced to abandon my investigation halfway through. I wasn't entirely clueless as to the murderer's identity, but I had to leave the actual solving of the mystery in someone else's hands.

Afterwards, I did everything I could to forget all about the events in question. So, when Hiroyuki Ishikari, the public prosecutor involved in the case, sent me a package containing a letter, a sealed note and a thick journal, I was practically dizzy with shock.

The journal revealed the true extent of the tragedy that had befallen the Chizui family. The role played by the Noh mask, and the frightful method by which the murders were carried out—it was all there, and in painstaking detail. Most remarkably of all, the entire account took the form of that new type of detective novel I had been vaguely aspiring to write—a detective memoir.

The journal—that of Koichi Yanagi, who in the end had been the one to solve the mysteries of the Chizui family—formed the bulk of the documents, with Mr Ishikari's letter providing an introduction and conclusion. They made for an enthralling read—but also an unsettling one. For they constituted a horrifying record of the damage that the crimes of a lunatic had inflicted on a great number of people, and precisely how those crimes had been exposed.

After careful consideration, I have decided to present these documents without the slightest embellishment. At this point, neither Mr Ishikari nor Koichi is likely to object. Certain moralizing types might well raise their eyebrows at my decision, but such prudishness has never held much weight with me.

However, on a personal level, the memoir is not exactly a comforting read. In it, Koichi coolly describes my every action, never hesitating to criticize them where he sees fit. The result, I have to say, is that I come across as a complete blundering idiot—hardly a flattering depiction, but so be it. My deductive talents are clearly no match for his, and anyway, in this particular case, we turned out to be approaching the incident from very different angles.

I'll end this preamble of mine here. The events described below took place in late August 1946, at the Chizui mansion, near the town of H– on the Miura peninsula in Kanagawa prefecture. Let us begin with Hiroyuki Ishikari's letter, which I present to you now.

1

An Uncanny Encounter on a Moonlit Night

(Hiroyuki Ishikari's letter)

Mr Takagi, it is already three months since you left the Chizui murder case in our hands and departed for Tokyo. Shortly after you left, the incident reached its cruel denouement. And with it, the tragedy of the Chizui family finally came to an end.

I feel I have a duty, to you at least, to reveal the truth behind that tragedy. Your friend, Koichi Yanagi, put his very life on the line trying to uncover the machinations of that monstrous criminal, and I believe this journal of his will provide you with an unforgettable record of those events.

When you left us, you told me that Koichi's journal could form the basis for a new type of detective novel, unprecedented anywhere in the world. Personally, I would rather you read it simply as the record of one man's blood and tears.

For an engineer, you turned out to be a surprisingly compassionate individual. This might sound a little impertinent, but I must confess a degree of jealousy regarding your ability to depart so abruptly from the Chizui mansion. You see, in my thirty years as a public prosecutor, my world has been governed by two things: crime, and the law. My task has been to divide human behaviour into categories that are black and white, and I have never been permitted to venture into the grey between. Four divided by two has always equalled two; to me, no other solution has ever been possible.

13

Even my colleagues call me a walking statute book; some liken me to a block of ice. Most other prosecutors allow some degree of personal emotion to creep into their application of the law. On occasion they apply their own discretion, and while the result may not always be some terrible upheaval of the social order, experience has shown me it never ends well. If I allowed my conscience to sway my application of the law even just once, I would feel obliged to resign from my role.

Of course, there's a reason I ended up this way. Thirty years ago, at this resort close to the town of H– on the Miura peninsula in Kanagawa prefecture, I fell in love with an exceedingly beautiful young woman. Her dewy skin, her glossy black hair, her tall, almost Grecian nose and her dark, dreamy eyes all seared themselves into the depths of my mind, where they have remained ever since. If our love had only reached a happier conclusion, I would never have spent the past three decades withering away like this—a single, ageing man so immersed in the law as to be barely even human.

But cruel fate wrenched us apart. After that one dreamlike and blissful summer, she slipped from my grasp forever. When I heard she was engaged to another man, I cried—cursing the world, cursing her. I endured many a sleepless night. At one point, I even contemplated killing both her and myself. But once my agitation and anguish had died down, I arrived at a sort of bitter resignation. The job of public prosecutor which awaited me came to seem like my one true calling. Still, the pain I'd experienced left a scar on my heart—one which I fear may never heal. Indeed, in the three decades since, I have never even experienced so much as another woman's rejection.

Mr Takagi, I wonder if you can understand how I felt upon being told I was being transferred to the public prosecutors' office in Yokohama, not far from the resort in question.

I am convinced that for every individual there is a place to which, no matter how much they might try to avoid it, they cannot help returning—a sort of spiritual home, if you like. Personally, this stretch of coast was the sacred site which I have never been able to forget. And, by a twist of fate, it was here that I became entangled in the bizarre case of the Chizui family murders, which marked the end of my thirty-year career as a prosecutor.

It was a humid evening in late August when, drawn to the beach by some mysterious force, I happened to stumble across Koichi Yanagi, the son of my departed friend, Genichiro.

That evening, grey thunderclouds towered on the horizon. No sooner had a damp gust of wind whistled past my cheeks than great drops of rain began thudding into the parched surface of the beach like a volley of pebbles, each leaving a black mark in its wake—then, moments later, they were violently pelting the roof of the small reed-walled hut where I had taken shelter. The horizon was soon shrouded in fog, and the four or five boats moored along the beach looked lonely and bereft in the downpour.

The storm kept up for around an hour. When the sky abruptly cleared and I finally left the hut, I was confronted by a breathtaking sight: an enormous double rainbow, arching in iridescent splendour across the heavens.

Most people will only see a handful of perfect double rainbows in their lifetime. As it happened, I had seen another one thirty years ago on this very beach, while I held that first love of mine in my arms. At the time, this rare phenomenon had seemed like some manifestation of a heavenly will, blessing our relationship and assuring our future happiness. With tears welling in our eyes, we had gazed wordlessly up at the sky.

I found myself walking along the rain-soaked shore in vague yet stubborn pursuit of the rainbow. Eventually, I cut across the sands and through a grove of red pines, until I found myself at the top of a sheer cliff overlooking the beach, where I stood gazing at the rainbows for what felt like an age. It was as though something inside me had finally given way; all the turbulent emotions I had spent the past three decades trying to repress came welling up in my chest. Before I knew it, warm tears were trickling down my cheeks.

But of course, rainbows are fleeting things. Before long, those glorious arcs had dissolved into the grey evening sky without a trace. It was only then that I came to my senses and, with a deep sigh, began to take in my surroundings.

Thirty years ago, there had been nothing here except pine trees, but at some point a patch had been cleared to make way for a stately Western-style mansion. Its grey walls had been darkened by years of exposure to the sea wind; and a pair of iron shutters, red with rust, guarded each of its windows, giving the entire building a vaguely brooding and secretive aspect. Houses have their own personalities. Or, at the very least, a house and its inhabitants cannot escape each other's mutual influence over their many years in each other's company. In which case, I thought to myself—who on earth might live in a mansion like this?

I approached the gate and peered at the plain wooden sign embedded in one of the crumbling red-brick gateposts. It bore the following name:

TAIJIRO CHIZUI

Chizui was not a common surname. In fact …

Just then, I heard footsteps approaching and turned around to find two large dark eyes staring at me. They belonged to a young man, perhaps thirty years of age. How could I have forgotten that broad, intelligent brow—or those melancholic yet resolute lips?

'Koichi, my boy!'

'Mr Ishikari!'

We spoke at almost the same instant.

His father, Genichiro, and I had been inseparable during our schooldays. And when Koichi was younger he, too, had often come over to my house after his classes, still wearing his black school cap with its distinctive white stripes. But all that was more than a decade ago. As fate would have it, his father had perished on the North Manchurian plains in the war, having taken poison to avoid capture. The young man standing before me was his only descendant.

At such moments we are apt to become sentimental. Unable to quell the sensation that I had somehow been reunited with Genichiro, I smiled in a bid to disguise the tears in my eyes.

'It's been rather a while, hasn't it?' said Koichi. 'I was repatriated from Burma not long ago. I'm sorry not to have been in touch. Where are you living these days, may I ask?'

'I was recently transferred to the Yokohama office. My house is on the outskirts of the city—not too far from here. What about you?'

'When I returned to Japan I was jobless and had nowhere to go. The Chizui family have been kind enough to let me live here with them. In exchange, I've been producing saccharin and dulcin in their laboratory for them to use as sweeteners.'

'Really? I'd never have imagined you'd be living *here*, of all places ...'

Perhaps these words of mine were not quite appropriate, or perhaps he was simply alarmed by the sudden excitement in my voice; whatever the reason, Koichi seemed rather taken aback.

17

'Is it so surprising?'

'Well, it's just I was reading the sign here just now, and the name reminded me of the Professor Chizui who died ten years ago. After all, Chizui isn't a very common surname, is it?'

'Ah, you knew of the Professor? Yes, this was his country retreat. When I was in high school, he was kind enough to act as my guarantor. That was what gave me the idea of coming here when I got back from the war.'

'I see … Koichi, there's so much to tell you, and even more to ask, but how about talking somewhere a little more comfortable? You could come over to my house tomorrow evening, perhaps?'

'I'd be delighted to. By the way, did you see that double rainbow just now? I suppose you're familiar with the German belief that any two lovers who see one of those together are doomed to separate. I'd never seen one before myself …'

I couldn't help wondering whether Koichi was himself in love. There was something about his words, and the way he gazed up at the sky across which the rainbow had until recently arched, that I found deeply affecting. I took my leave of him and, feeling strangely unsettled, hurried away from the mansion.

As we'd agreed, Koichi paid me a visit the next evening. After an hour or so of innocuous chatter, I steered the conversation around to the topic that had been weighing on my mind.

'Tell me, how exactly did Professor Chizui die?'

'A heart attack. He was in the middle of an experiment when a glass flask exploded. His injuries left him bedridden, and shortly afterwards his heart failed. But, Mr Ishikari, something tells me his death was no mere accident.'

'Well, I'm not sure about that—but it was certainly a great loss. Not being a scientist myself, I can't speak for his specific achievements, but he was a brilliant researcher, wasn't he? I've heard people say he deserved a Nobel.'

'Indeed. Western scientists are only now, ten years after his death, acknowledging the true value of what he accomplished. The Professor was a worldwide authority on radiochemistry. If he'd lived and been provided with adequate facilities and funding, I dare say Japan might have beaten America to the atomic bomb. But of course, that wasn't to be ...'

'How is his family these days?'

I had asked my question quite nonchalantly, but Koichi's expression immediately soured.

'The Professor's wife lost her mind soon after he passed away; she's been a patient at the Oka Asylum in Tokyo ever since. And to think that when I was a student she doted on me like her own child ... As you know, I was struggling to pay my tuition fees back then and ended up taking a job as a tutor to Hisako, the Professor's daughter. Hisako had been known for her beauty and virtuosic piano playing ever since her school-days. But it seems that while I was away in the army, her sanity unravelled completely—though whether her madness came from her mother or some other cause, I don't know. When I came to see her shortly after I returned, I was shocked to find her barely a shadow of her former self.

'But the tragedy of the Chizui family doesn't end there. The Professor's only son, Kenkichi, now fourteen years old, is in good mental health, but he's been diagnosed with heart valve disease. It seems he doesn't have long to live—and yet nobody has told him. It brings a tear to my eyes whenever I see him poring over his textbooks in preparation for his middle-school entry exams. It seems that, before long, there will be no one left to carry the torch of Professor Chizui's genius.'

Koichi silently lowered his head. I could only share his grief.

'So who else lives in the house now?'

'The Professor's younger brother, Taijiro, brought his family here after they were burned out of their home in the Tokyo firebombing.' At this point, Koichi's voice seemed to flare with anger. 'Mr Ishikari, I hate to speak ill of the people who have taken me into their home, but there is something deeply wrong with Taijiro's entire branch of the family.

'Take Taijiro, the head of the family: he is possessed by the most malign greed. The blood of Judas, who betrayed Christ for the mere sake of some silver, might well be pulsing through his veins. There's no telling what he might do to satisfy his lust for wealth. In fact, I'm sure he'd be perfectly happy to murder someone—as long as it didn't put him in danger personally.

'His elder son, Rintaro, is a terrifying nihilist. All he really believes in is power; to him, justice and morality are no more than intellectual games. He seems to view everything in this world as a sort of dreary mirage, contemplating reality in the indifferent way one might gaze at a passing cloud in the sky. All capacity for feeling has deserted him, leaving behind only his abnormally sharp intellect; if he hasn't murdered anyone yet, it's probably only because it doesn't agree with him as a hobby. He told me as much himself once, in no uncertain terms. If it had been you he was talking to, I imagine he would have informed you, with a scornful smile, that "the ultimate law is lawlessness itself".

'It's the same with Taijiro's second son, Yojiro. He may not be quite as craven as his father, but still—a snake only ever begets a snake. If we were to compare Taijiro to a mighty sword, Yojiro is more like a dagger glinting in its sheath.

'Even Taijiro's mother, Sonoe, long bedridden with palsy, has the same fiery temper smouldering away inside her. And while his daughter, Sawako, is the most reasonably minded of the family, you have to remember that for many years she has had only lunatics, near-lunatics and invalids for company. Who knows when she might succumb to some violent fit of emotion?

'Between the two remaining members of the Professor's own family, and these five members of Taijiro's branch, it is safe to say there is no love lost. As Jules Renard once put it, a family is a group of people living under the same roof who cannot stand each other. That house has been struck by a disease from within. Riven by mutual hatred, suspicion and a sheer failure to understand one another, the Chizuis are engaged in a perpetual and desperate struggle.

'But precisely because their respective forces have reached a sort of equilibrium, the family appears, on the surface at least, to be entirely at peace. Any disruption of that balance, however momentary, would surely spell the downfall of the entire family. Who knows what tragedy may erupt among that forsaken tribe? In any case, I fear it may be fast approaching ...'

His voice was crackling with emotion. I found myself wondering whether he had spent so long among the warped people he was describing that he might be beginning to harbour his own visceral hatred for them.

And yet his harsh words turned out to be true. A terrifying secret lurked within the Chizui family. As you will see from his journal, it was Koichi, with his outstanding skills of deduction, who, before our very eyes, penetrated that secret and solved the murders so brilliantly. At the same time, it wouldn't be long before every single member of this once-noble family had departed from this world.

A few days later, on the night of a full moon, Koichi invited me to a festival in the nearby fishing town of K–. As I had no wife or children of my own, and Koichi no parents or other relatives to speak of, a sort of familial intimacy had sprung up between us.

The scene that presented itself at the festival was almost exactly the same as I remembered it from thirty years ago—fireworks, lanterns, shabby food stalls—and yet the face of my companion back then, asking me to wait while she bought me a whelk egg case, had been lost to the winds of time ...

Eventually Koichi and I made our way out of the crowd and began walking home. The moonlight broke softly on the rippled surface of the sea, suffusing the entire scene with a silvery glow. As we passed through the grove of pine trees, their red trunks wet with dew, our footsteps were muffled, as though the sound had been absorbed into some other realm.

Just as we were approaching the promontory on which the Chizui mansion stood, I heard the mournful sound of a piano. I believe it was Liszt's Sixth Hungarian Rhapsody, which even under normal circumstances tends to leave the listener feeling somewhat crazed. But that night, I perceived something monstrous and otherworldly in the melody.

Koichi nodded silently at my side. As I had guessed, we were listening to the playing of a madwoman. Hisako Chizui, once renowned for her brilliance at the piano, was grasping at the fraying threads of her memory in order to perform the rhapsody.

For a moment, we simply stood there and listened.

Then we saw it.

A demonic face had appeared in one of the upstairs windows, leering at us in the light of the full moon ...

This was no illusion, and nor were we hallucinating. Even from a distance, we could clearly make out the sharp fangs and horns, bathed in cold moonlight. On that pale and wrathful face, the eyes alone glittered gold, while the cleft-like mouth that stretched almost from one ear to the other, looked as though it had, only a moment ago, been sucking the blood of some poor victim.

We could still hear the piano. In fact, the melody began to accelerate, becoming all the more terrifying, the notes racing towards us from somewhere behind the demon in the window. Soon all sense of rhythm had disappeared; the playing spiralled out of tune, straying from any musical scale. It was as though the awful cackle of the demon itself was being borne to us on the wind.

Then the piano abruptly stopped. In its place, the ghastly, deranged laughter of a woman pierced the night air.

The face was still visible in the window.

It was a deeply unnerving scene. But my prosecutorial instincts had taken over, and I saw in it not some fantastical nightmare, but confirmation that a complex web of secrets and conspiracy surely lurked within the Chizui family.

'Do you see that, Koichi?'

'Yes. A demon ...'

'A real one, you think?'

'Surely not. No, it must be the Noh mask that's kept in the house. It's been handed down through the family for over two centuries. The story goes that a Noh actor named Gennojo Hosho once cursed it, and now it harbours his evil spirit. But ... who could be wearing it at this time of night?'

His voice was trembling like he'd been doused with cold water. Just then, the demon withdrew silently from the window.

'Koichi, I realize now that I should have taken you more seriously. As a prosecutor, I can't help sensing that this bizarre scene may be the prelude to a terrible crime. Unless … could it have been Hisako wearing that mask?'

'Impossible,' replied Koichi quickly, his voice trembling with a mixture of tension and fear. 'You see, while the mask is kept in a case in the same room as the piano, only Taijiro has the key. Anyway, the music was still playing when the demon appeared in the window, but the piano and that window are separated by quite a distance. There's no way it could be her.'

'Listen,' I told him, 'I need to get to the bottom of this. I hate to intrude, but I'd like to speak with the master of the house. Could you go and see if he's free?'

Koichi nodded and disappeared into the back entrance.

I was increasingly convinced that, before long, a dreadful crime was going to occur in this house. The bizarre scene we had just witnessed was probably only the overture …

I stood there, a cigarette dangling unlit from my mouth, as I gazed steadily at the dark, shadowy form of the mansion.

Eventually Koichi returned. His voice trembled as he spoke.

'Taijiro says he can see you now.'

The front door opened slightly, casting a square of yellow light onto the ground in front of it. And so it was that I first crossed the threshold of the Chizui mansion—the stage of the awful tragedy to come.

The maid who had let me in guided me to a lavish reception room, where I waited for a few minutes until the door quietly opened.

'My apologies for the wait. Taijiro Chizui.'

A grey-haired man with a slight stoop walked into the room. He must have been about sixty.

Here he was: the only sibling of the genius Professor Chizui. And yet nothing in his expression seemed indicative of the passionate yearning for knowledge that had so characterized his older brother. I'd heard he'd been a doctor with his own private medical practice for many years, and yet his demeanour was more reminiscent of some craven shopkeeper, with no trace of the dignified resolve usually associated with men of his profession. If his face suggested anything, it was a startling capacity for greed and malice. He had a large, hooked nose, small eyes that darted around relentlessly behind his gold-rimmed spectacles, thick lips, a heavy double chin, an unappealingly vague smile and a low, insidious voice.

I had known a defendant once—a dentist who had taken out a hefty insurance policy on his wife's life, then poisoned her and eloped with his lover, before eventually being arrested. Something about the man before me reminded me of that dentist. If Professor Chizui had shunned all external distractions in his relentless quest for knowledge, I got the impression his brother instead simply saw knowledge as a tool for acquiring wealth, and would be willing to go to any lengths for personal gain.

'I'm sorry to bother you so late in the evening—Hiroyuki Ishikari, from the Yokohama District Public Prosecutors' Office. Koichi and I were walking past your mansion just now, and we happened to witness some rather mysterious goings-on upstairs. I just wanted to ask a few questions.'

'I see,' he replied, settling into a chair. 'And what might these mysterious goings-on have been?'

'We saw a demon.'

For a brief moment, Taijiro's features seemed to twitch with anxiety.

'Do you mean a real demon? Or perhaps someone in a mask … ?'

'Not a real one, of course—not in this day and age. But I hear you have a cursed mask in the family—handed down over two centuries, I'm told? Now, I don't mean to pry into your family's private affairs, but do you have any idea who might have appeared in the window wearing that terrifying object this late at night—or why?'

Taijiro was visibly shaken. He rose from his chair as if attempting to conceal his trepidation; his voice trembled as he spoke.

'If Koichi has already gone and told you, I suppose there's no point trying to hide anything. Yes, that *hannya* mask, crafted by the great Ittosai Akazuru, is our family heirloom. Previously it was passed down the main branch of our family—that of the Marquis Yoshida, the *daimyo* of Hokuetsu. But it is also the subject of a terrifying legend ...

'Around two hundred years ago, a young Noh actor, whom the family had taken into service, fell in love with one of the lord's maids. But she never returned his affections. Indeed, quite the opposite: she revealed his secret to the entire household, rendering him a complete laughing stock. The actor fell into a deep depression. After donning that mask and giving a final performance of the play *Dojoji* in front of the lord, he took poison and ended his life. Soon afterwards, the maid went mad, and the mask was never used in performance again. Rumours spread that it harboured a terrible and powerful curse. If you wore it on the night of a full moon and recited a certain phrase, your wish would be granted—but in exchange, you'd be forced to give up your own life, just like the original wearer ... So, Mr Ishikari, you're telling me someone in this house was wearing the mask this evening?'

By now, Taijiro seemed gripped by an uncontrollable fear.

'Where is it kept?' I asked.

'A glass case in the spare room upstairs.'

'And who has the key?'

26

'I do.'

'Would you mind showing me it?'

'Of course not. Follow me.'

He led us down the hall and up the large staircase to the left of the front door. We came to a halt by the first room on the left at the top of the stairs.

'It's in here,' he said, flicking a light switch.

As we stepped into the Western-style room, an eerie sight immediately confronted us. From the glass case mounted on a table by the wall glared the cursed mask—and yet that was not the most shocking thing in the room. In the corner, hunched over a black piano, was the deranged Hisako.

As soon as the light came on, she rose to her feet and turned to stare vacantly at us. It was just as Koichi had warned me: madness seemed to have oddly accentuated her beauty, lending her the uncanny allure of a wild rose blooming out of season. But there was something wax-like and cold about her expression; her long, dishevelled hair hung loosely over her shoulders, and the dark pupils of her large eyes stirred so restlessly that it was impossible to know exactly what, if anything, was the target of her gaze.

She advanced a few paces towards us. Her face was as expressionless as that of a wax figure or a Noh mask, and yet she appeared to be murmuring something over and over. Then, before I knew what was happening, she had lunged at me and pressed herself to my chest.

'Finally!' she whooped. 'You're back! I'll never let you go, you hear? You're mine for ever!'

It had been three decades since I had last known a woman's embrace, and even then I'd never experienced anything like this. At the same time, it was quite a terrifying encounter. I simply stood there, powerless to stop the complex whirl of emotions—fear and pity, dread and faint nostalgia—that had stirred inside me.

But it really was only a moment, for Taijiro immediately grabbed Hisako by the shoulders and pulled her from my chest.

'What are you playing at? This man is our guest, not that lover of yours. *He* died a very long time ago, and he's never coming back, you hear?'

It wasn't clear whether she had understood him. At first, she simply fixed her vacant gaze on me again. But soon an unsettling smile began to tug at the corners of her lips.

From a vase on top of the piano, she picked out a single carnation and brought it to her mouth. Then she abruptly began to sing:

> *My heart goes south to find you;*
> *My letter entrusted to a swallow,*
> *Alone, I wait out the winter,*
> *When, oh, when, will you return?*

It was a poignant melody, reminiscent of some old German ballad. As she sang, she wandered off down the hallway, but the melancholy tune seemed to linger faintly in the air.

Taijiro also appeared to have been listening keenly. He turned to me with a bitter smile.

'I'm sorry, that must have been quite alarming. Hisako is a little … unbalanced, you see. She's my brother's daughter, but if anything she seems to have taken after her mother. She was all but engaged to a young nobleman, but then he died in the war—and now look at her.'

Koichi and I remained silent, immersed in our thoughts. The sight of that once-talented and beautiful woman, now

28

consumed by madness, seemed to have deeply moved him; I could I have sworn I saw tears glistening in his eyes.

After a short pause, we managed to gather ourselves.

'So,' I said, 'this is the Noh mask you were telling me about.'

'Indeed.'

Taijiro had not lied: the mask was indeed a terrifying piece of craftsmanship. The large, sharply upturned golden eyes; the crescent-shaped mouth that extended almost to the ears, its sharp fangs protruding from either side; the long, subtly curved horns—it was all enough to stop anyone dead in their tracks. Could that young Noh actor's final grudge really still lurk in the mask now, two hundred years after his death?

I slowly put a hand to the lid of the case.

'So it's kept locked ... The key, please. Tell me, do you keep it on you at all times?'

'Well, not always.'

'I wonder if someone could have taken the key when you weren't looking, made a duplicate and used it to open this just now ...'

As I spoke, I unlocked the case and carefully retrieved the mask—but at that very moment, something happened that made us freeze on the spot.

The lights went out in an instant; it was a power cut. Now, only pale moonlight flooded through the windows, casting half of the cursed mask's surface into eerie shadow—and just then, I heard that sinister laugh again. For a moment, it seemed to be coming from the mask in my hand.

It was a wonder I didn't drop it to the floor. The silence that reigned in the mansion had been broken by the piercing laughter of the deranged Hisako, reverberating manically down the hallway as if in mockery of our terror.

29

My dear Mr Takagi, all this was only the prelude to the affair. At this point, I had not yet grasped quite how unsettling and bizarre this case would turn out to be. The events that night turned out to form a crucial prologue to the tragedy of the Chizui family—and yet it was only much later that I understood their true significance.

I ask that you read the rest of this story directly from Koichi's journal. Until the final stages of the investigation, I was really no more than a bystander. When you have read his account—which takes a format unprecedented in any detective novel in the world, as you excitedly claimed it would—please return to this letter of mine. Then, finally, please open the sealed note that I have also enclosed. Only then, my dear Mr Takagi, will my true intentions become clear to you.

2

Opening Act

(Koichi Yanagi's journal)

I began keeping this journal at the suggestion of Hiroyuki Ishikari, the public prosecutor. Now that I think about it, I wonder if our chance meeting by the Chizui mansion—Mr Ishikari having ventured there in pursuit of a double rainbow—could have somehow been the work of my father guiding us from beyond the grave. And, with the appearance of that masked figure on a moonlit night, he fell, like me, under the grip of the secrets of the Chizui family.

That night he left the mansion unable to conceal his consternation.

'Have you ever studied Noh?' he asked me, as I accompanied him part of the way home. 'You haven't? Well, perhaps I should briefly enlighten you. After all, Noh has an undisputed claim to be the most refined form of masked theatre in the world. Even the symbolic dramas of Yeats, that giant of modern Irish literature, bear quite a stunning resemblance to Noh.

'But what I want to tell you now concerns the Noh mask itself, and its enigmatic appearance. Now, for a play to achieve the status of high art, it is of course important that its characters can express the whole gamut of human emotion. Even in the Joruri plays of the *Bunraku* puppet theatre, renowned for being the most refined of their kind in the world, the puppets are skilfully constructed to achieve this: their eyebrows, eyes and mouth can each be moved independently by the puppeteer.

'But the Noh mask allows for no such movement. In theatre, there are two methods of conveying the basic attributes of the characters—for example, whether they are young or old, male or female: either by using masks, or by applying make-up to the actors' faces. The abrupt decline of other forms of masked theatre was in no small part due to the inability of masks to express changes in emotions.

'But in Noh, this problem is solved through a stunning refinement of technique. Firstly, because the plays are heavily symbolic in nature, and unfold in a dreamlike manner, the expressionlessness of the Noh mask is no hindrance to performance. Indeed, you could even say that its very lack of expression is what enables it to express such a wide range of emotion.

'A second factor is the sheer craftsmanship of the mask itself. With the Noh masks depicting female characters, the actor tilts the mask upwards to smile, and downwards to cry. Seen from the front, it is possible to convey quite clearly an expression of joy or sadness.

'Now, you may have heard how in Kabuki theatre, the transition from candlelight to electric light made it extremely difficult for the *onnagata*—the male actors playing female roles, that is—to act their parts. The harsh lighting revealed their wrinkles, ruining the illusion of their femininity. It was the same with Noh: watching it under the electric lights of a modern theatre, the effect is quite different from what was originally intended. You see, during the Muromachi period— the golden age of Noh—the stage would only have been lit from one direction.

'It is a technique that is still used in the Takigi school of Noh in Nara. On the lawn in front of Kofuku-ji temple, you will find an ancient open-air stage on which Noh is regularly performed. On the day of a performance, monks dressed in black warrior robes gather on the stone steps leading to the temple to watch the play. The sounds of the accompanying instruments—flute, *taiko* and hand drums—are carried by the wind through the pine trees and up into the Tobihino sky, and when the evening sun eventually descends behind the gentle Nara mountains, a ceremonial curtain is raised in front of the temple. The monks, bearing wooden torches, proceed to kindle a stack of firewood prepared in advance. The Noh performance continues deep into the night—with the stage illuminated by the fierce flames of the bonfire. Witnessing such a performance may well be the only way of truly appreciating the profound beauty of Noh. Lit only from one side by the red firelight, the masks seem to harbour beautiful and mysterious depths. That, Koichi, is how they are supposed to be viewed.'

'Well, Mr Ishikari, that was quite an education. But what's the connection with the events of this evening?'

'My dear Koichi, don't you see? When we first saw the mask in the window, and again when the lights went out, we saw it only by the oblique light of the moon. Didn't that sight leave you breathless with fear?'

I found myself nodding firmly in agreement.

'Now, you may not have noticed this, but there are always slight differences in the expression between the left and right sides of a *hannya* mask. In almost every Noh play, the demon is eventually exorcized by a venerable priest and achieves spiritual peace through the power of Buddhism. As a result, even the most severe-looking mask will bear on one side a slight expression of redemption. At the end of the play, the actor will subtly draw attention to that side of the mask in order to emphasize the demon's newfound peace. But I could see no trace of redemption on the mask we saw tonight, Koichi—no matter how hard I looked.'

I had seen the mask many times before, and it had never failed to unsettle me profoundly. Now, for the first time, I understood why.

'Malediction, vindictiveness, spite—those are the only emotions it seems capable of conveying. You know, I imagine it wasn't simply a coincidence that it stopped being used in performance.

'The other thing to remember is that in Noh, of course, the masks always prevent us from seeing the actors' faces. In this sense, it differs fundamentally from the cinema or regular theatre.

'Sometimes we may be seized by a desire to see the face of the actor behind the mask. It is not unheard of for the leading actor to appear without a mask—a practice known as *hitamen*—but even then, their face will remain completely expressionless throughout the performance, almost as if it were itself a mask.

'Unnatural façades have a habit of concealing sinister intentions. What secrets might be lurking behind that mask? I want to know who was wearing it. I want to see the face of the person who donned that terrifying object on this moonlit night. Mark my words: the Chizui household harbours some awful secret ...

'You must stay alert, Koichi. You've always been the observant, analytical type: I hope you'll use those skills now to discover this family's secrets. I don't know what, precisely, is going to happen next, but tragedy is in the air. Indeed, we may be powerless to stop it—in which case our task shall simply be to keep the bloodshed to a minimum.'

Mr Ishikari stopped to light his cigarette. Bathed from head to toe in pale moonlight, he turned and stared back at the Chizui mansion for the longest time.

It was true: a terrible plot was afoot in the Chizui household. Ever since the Professor's death, a dark, hidden current had coursed through the family, threatening to erupt at any moment—a danger that loomed closer and closer with every passing day. Now, with the appearance of the demon on that moonlit night, the stage was set for the tragedy to unfold.

When I visited Mr Ishikari the next day, he seemed unusually animated.

'Koichi, I'm convinced there's a secret at the heart of that family. You see, I had a look through the reports from the Professor's death ten years ago, and there's something about them that troubles me ... In any case, I don't think that was the end of the story. Koichi, for the sake of justice and decency, I want you to keep a record of everything you observe over the coming days. When, as seems likely, some kind of incident occurs, an account of that sort will be invaluable.'

And so it was that I began writing this journal.

In the end, we only had to wait until the following day for the incident Mr Ishikari had feared. An invisible killer took Taijiro's life without anyone even noticing. The room in which the victim was found had been fully sealed; the murderer had carried out a bizarre vanishing act. All that greeted us was the cold, empty stare of the Noh mask lying on the floor; it seemed almost to laugh in the face of the terror that filled the household.

Ever since our sighting of the demon in the window, Taijiro had seemed gripped by an unspeakable fear. The entire family had been home that evening—and one of them had, undoubtedly, been wearing the mask. Perhaps he had already vaguely surmised who it was; at any rate, he seemed convinced that, if

35

he *was* going to be killed in his sleep, it would be by whoever had worn the mask.

And yet he seemed unable to reveal his suspicions to anyone. His wife had already passed away; he was not comfortable confiding in his own children. He'd made me swear not to tell anyone else about the appearance of the masked figure in the window, instead preferring to embark on his own tortured hunt for the truth.

However, this mental agony soon became more than he could bear. Two days after the mask had appeared in the window, at around eight o'clock in the evening, he summoned me to his room.

'Koichi, you wouldn't happen to know a decent private detective, would you?'

I glanced at him in surprise. What was he so frightened of, I wondered—and what was he trying to find out?

'I can't say I do—but if there's something you're worried about, wouldn't it be better to go to the police instead?'

'If this were an external matter, I'd be happy to. But, Koichi, a family as illustrious as ours has its pride and reputation to consider. If an actual crime had been committed, that would be one thing—but if I go to the police with nothing but a vague fear to report, they'll probably just laugh at me. Someone wearing a mask isn't exactly evidence of an impending murder. Still, I can't shake the feeling that something is afoot. I keep imagining that mask staring at me from outside my window at night—it's enough to give me the shivers. I probably shouldn't be telling you this, but there's no one in this family I can trust. No one at all! I don't trust the police, either. There's simply no one I can turn to for help.'

'What about discussing the matter with Mr Ishikari—the gentleman who was with me the other evening?'

'Him? Not a chance. Public prosecutors are lowly creatures, Koichi. They're barely able to pick up the pieces in the wake of a crime, never mind prevent one from occurring in the first place.'

Just then, a name occurred to me. Akimitsu Takagi. How could I have forgotten my old school friend? After studying metallurgical engineering, Akimitsu had abandoned that field entirely and devoted himself to reading detective novels from around the world. He even fancied himself an amateur investigator and had asked me to let him know about any incidents that might allow him to put his deductive skills to practical use.

He also happened to have relocated to this very stretch of coast for the summer, and was staying a mere fifteen minutes' walk away, at the Marine Hotel. He was your average member of the leisured class—the type of layabout I normally couldn't stand—but I also knew him through and through. In terms of brains and practical competence at least, he was perfectly suited to the job.

'Wait,' I said, slapping my thigh enthusiastically, 'I *do* know someone—just the man for your purposes, in fact. An old schoolmate of mine, Akimitsu Takagi—he's intelligent, courageous, and as persistent as anyone you could ever meet. He's read just about any detective novel he's been able to lay his hands on, and even fancies himself Japan's answer to Philo Vance. He used to demonstrate his flair by solving the occasional minor mystery at school. He has no money to speak of, but plenty of time on his hands, so as long as we present the case to him in a manner that, well, the phrase "tickles his interest" hardly seems appropriate, but … intrigues him, he'll be sure to lend a hand. To top it all off, he's staying just fifteen minutes from here. What do you say?'

Taijiro seemed to share my enthusiasm. 'Yes, he sounds perfect. Go and ask him at once, would you?'

'Certainly. I'll just phone him.'

I left the room and made my way downstairs. As I did so, I passed that monster, Rintaro Chizui, coming the other way.

Monster—that was the only word to describe him. He was probably a genius, too, at least as far as mental acuity was concerned—and yet I felt reluctant to apply that label to any intellect so devoid of emotion. One might equally be tempted to call him superhuman. But was it really right to bestow that title on someone so deeply uninterested in human life, someone so completely unmoved by our existence, or by the art, passions or even crimes of which we are capable; a man who saw in everything only a void; a man who scorned not only morality, but also the material world and humanity itself; a man, in short, who was as lifeless as cold ash?

Still, I couldn't deny that there was a strange, nihilistic incisiveness about everything he said and did. When I had first arrived at the Chizui residence after the war, he had greeted me with extraordinary coldness:

'So, Koichi—a bit better at killing people now, are you? Still, there's nothing quite so idiotic as war. All those millions of lives extinguished for nothing—and each soldier forced to gamble his own life against the enemy's. What an unappealing way to go about murdering people … If it were me, I'd choose a more sure-fire method, and kill however many people I felt like. And I don't say that because I hold my own life particularly dear. I just hate the idea of sharing a level playing field with my opponent. That's why I avoided joining the army—I simply couldn't endure the worm-like existence of a soldier. It was simply a question of pulling the right strings …'

At his words I had felt a surge of anger. I am no militarist or advocate of war, but to be rewarded with a sermon like that, after all those gruelling years at the front, came as a real jolt.

As he passed me now, his face was eerily illuminated by the light at the top of the stairs. He stopped and looked me up and down with those restless, searching eyes of his—the only lively feature on his otherwise pale and expressionless face—before disappearing wordlessly into his father's room, from which I had just emerged. He had what looked like a camera case slung over the shoulder of his open-necked shirt.

The encounter left me rather unsettled, but I gathered myself and continued downstairs to the telephone booth by the front door. I managed to get Akimitsu on the line, and he listened eagerly as I explained Taijiro's request.

As we talked, I couldn't shake the feeling that someone was lurking outside. I even thought I heard the faint rustling of a kimono. But when I opened the door of the booth and glanced up and down the hall, it was deserted. I felt increasingly disconcerted. By now all I wanted to do was to see Akimitsu in person as soon as possible.

I had finished the call and was about to head back upstairs when a voice from behind stopped me in my tracks.

'Koichi, do you have a moment?'

It was Sawako. She must have been the one hiding in the hallway.

In this family of the deranged and ill, the presence of a woman as demure as Sawako Chizui was almost baffling. Her grandmother was half-paralysed down one side of her body; she had a lunatic for a cousin, a money-grubber for a father and a nihilist for a brother—had any ordinary woman been left to fend for herself among such people, she would surely have been reduced to nothing but an empty shell.

And yet Sawako's youthful vitality had ably withstood this pressure. Her placid, noble features would occasionally flicker into life as some long-repressed emotion darted across them with all the fleetingness of a shooting star.

But from the cold treatment she received at the hands of her father and brothers, you'd hardly have thought they were even related. In her twenty-eight years, she had never been permitted to love or marry, but was simply expected to carry out her duties as the lady of the house—though in fact, her role was often no more than that of a glorified maid. It seemed no one in the family had ever even thought of finding her a husband. Thus, while she might initially appear to be on an equal footing with the rest of them, in reality she was little more than a slave condemned to a life of endless toil.

She was gazing pleadingly at me; her beautiful face was damp with sweat. The thin eyebrows she was normally so careful to cover with eyebrow pencil were bare and arched with sadness. I could feel her warm breath on my face.

'Koichi, I'm begging you: leave this house. Get away from here as soon as you can.'

I stared at her in surprise. She had always been kinder than the others to me—had welcomed me back from the war with open arms. Why, all of a sudden, was she telling me to leave?

'I can't explain—not now. But I fear something terrible is going to happen. That awful mask appears in my dreams every night. I feel it glaring at us both. Last night, too—I dreamed you were falling headlong into this awful, deep morass. I reached out a hand to help you, but it was no use: your face had morphed into that of a terrifying monster. Pale will-o'-the-wisps danced around the swamp, flickering in the darkness. I could only cry and listen to the harsh roar of the wind—and, from the depths of the abyss into which you had fallen, your distant, plaintive groaning. At that point, I awoke from sheer horror.

'This house is no place for a man like you, Koichi. Until now, your presence has brought me comfort. But you simply can't stay here. Something awful is about to happen—I just know it. I am begging you, flee—and take me with you. Please. I can't bear it here. I feel like I'm suffocating … Please, Koichi! Help me!'

Sawako had always seemed so unsusceptible to any sort of emotion. But these words of hers sounded for all the world like those of someone desperately in love.

'Sawako, please! I'm a scientist—you can hardly expect me to give much credence to a dream, no matter how vivid. Anyway, eloping with a wretch like me, with no home or employment of my own, would be a breach of your family's trust. Just think how your father would feel! No, Sawako—you deserve far better than me.'

'But, Koichi, don't you see? This is the only way we both make it out of this alive. Our last chance. Please—won't you reconsider?'

I didn't know what else to say to her. Clearly, Sawako knew something, and was using this dream of hers as a pretext to get me away from the house. I felt this intuitively to be the case. And yet under the circumstances, I could hardly do as she suggested.

'I'll think it over, all right?'

'You just don't get it, do you? There's no *time*, Koichi!'

She gave me a tormented look. I glanced away and, with a quick bow, wordlessly escaped up the stairs. I could feel her behind me, gazing worriedly at me, as though she had more to say.

Just as I raised my hand to knock on the door of Taijiro's room, I heard the cold voice of Rintaro from inside.

'You really want to take her out? After everything? All our efforts will have been for nothing. Well, as you please. It's all rather ridiculous, anyway.'

'I'm telling you,' came Taijiro's faint reply, 'something bad is going to happen. I don't know what, exactly, but I can feel it. I really do think, for my own safety as much as anything, that getting rid of her is the only way to proceed.'

Then the two seemed to lower their voices; I was unable to hear any more. Rather than interrupt, I decided to look in on Kenkichi and Hisako, whose room neighboured Taijiro's. Hisako was already asleep in her bed, but I found Kenkichi awake. After exchanging a few words with him, I left the room and, finally, knocked on Taijiro's door.

When I walked in I found the two sitting down, still deep in discussion. Seeing me, Rintaro immediately got to his feet.

'Perhaps we should talk again tomorrow, Father. Goodnight.'

With a cold glance in my direction, he left the room. He seemed to be heading for the darkroom in the attic, where he spent a lot of time developing photos.

'Well, Koichi, did you manage to speak to Mr Takagi?' asked Taijiro anxiously.

'Yes. Don't worry—he agreed to take the case. I'll drop by his hotel right now. Would you be willing to write a formal letter requesting his services?'

'Of course. Just a moment.'

He turned to his desk and began scribbling away. Stifled by the heat, I looked around the room and realized why. The windows were shut tight; even the iron shutters outside were closed. The only openings were the series of small pivot windows installed just above the main windows for ventilation purposes. A fan whirred dully in the room.

I relieved him of the letter and left the room. It was twenty past eight in the evening. After dropping by Hisako and Kenkichi's room for a few minutes, I made my way directly to the Marine Hotel.

I found Akimitsu in a room that looked out onto the sea, sitting in an armchair where, as usual, he was devouring one of his beloved detective novels. This was his daily occupation, and his only real hobby.

Even during our schooldays, I'd always found it quite hard to respect Akimitsu. He had the unfortunate habit of always wanting to contradict you: if you said left, he said right; if you said white, he said black. What's more, he never backed down, stubbornly clinging to his assertions until he got his way. Whenever I warned him about this habit, he simply ignored me, boasting instead about his superior intellect and cultivated mind. On a not insignificant number of occasions, I had considered breaking off our friendship altogether.

'What's that you're reading?'

'Oh, this? *The Greene Murder Case*, by the great Van Dine. I've read it countless times, but it never fails to entertain me.'

He was looking at me ironically from behind the thick spectacles he wore for his short-sightedness. He had a prominent, slightly curved nose, thick, bushy eyebrows, a large mouth and the same tousled mop of hair he'd had as a student.

'I'm here about the matter we discussed on the phone. Mr Chizui, the master of the house where I'm staying, wants to enlist your services. You see, there was quite a bizarre turn of events at the house the night before last, and he's been rather jittery ever since. He's convinced something bad is about to happen and wants a private detective on the case. I recommended you—are you up to it? Here's his letter.'

He looked sharply up at me through his glasses, then opened the envelope. Tilting the shade of the green lamp at his side, he silently perused its contents.

'What a peculiar request. The man is clearly hiding something. From both the content and the handwriting I detect a sort of vague fear—a feeling of anxiety in the face of a mysterious threat. He may not know exactly what form that threat will take, but he knows he has ample grounds to be afraid. Koichi, I have to say I'm quite fascinated by this letter—or at least by its author's frantic state of mind. You must tell me more. I want all the details!'

Just as he turned to face me, the telephone on his desk rang. I instinctively looked at the clock: it was ten minutes to nine.

'It's for you,' he said, handing me the receiver.

'Koichi, it's me, Taijiro. Did you meet Mr Takagi? You see, just after you left, something rather ghastly happened. That demon appeared again! I finally learned who was behind the mask ...'

'Well, who was it?'

'I can't tell you now. Put Mr Takagi on, would you?'

I handed the receiver to Akimitsu.

'Hello? Yes, this is Takagi. Thank you for your letter—it sounds as though you're rather worried. I'm not sure how much use I'll be, but I'll be happy to help. What's that? You want me to come over right this minute? That's a bit sudden, don't you think ... What? You know who was wearing the mask, and there isn't a moment to spare? Well, who was it? You can't tell me over the phone ... Very well, I'll be over right away. Twenty minutes at the most. See you shortly.'

Akimitsu replaced the receiver and got to his feet.

'Come on, Koichi. That was all quite alarming! We must find out who was wearing that mask as soon as we can. Everything else can wait.'

He hurried me out of the room. As we made our way to the Chizui mansion, he urged me to tell him everything that had happened since the night before last. He listened wordlessly, his lips tightly compressed, his pace gradually quickening as we walked.

'Yes, something is certainly afoot,' he murmured when I'd finished. 'A dark secret must lurk in the family. I suspect they all know what it is, but they're too terrified to speak out—yes, they must be possessed by some unspeakable fear …'

Soon the large, gloomy outline of the mansion came into view on the promontory. We were almost there. Taijiro's windows were visible from the path. But the iron shutters were still closed, and only faint light came from the pivot windows above them.

We stood at the entrance and rang the bell. Its chime echoed briefly through the mansion's slumbering interior before fading again.

Then we heard it. A piercing, high-pitched scream, more like that of some wild beast than human. It seemed to come from upstairs.

We stood rooted to the spot. Under the glow of the porch lamp, Akimitsu's face had turned pale. He continued frantically ringing the bell while I began pounding on the door.

The maid who eventually opened the door looked queasy with anxiety.

'What was that scream?' I asked, cutting to the chase.

'Afraid I don't know, sir. It may've been Miss Hisako.'

'No, I don't think so,' Akimitsu interjected. 'Didn't sound like a woman. Is your master home?'

45

'Yes, sir. In his room upstairs, I believe.'

The maid seemed to want to add something, but this was no time for explanations. We brushed her to one side and raced up the front stairs. We were greeted in the hall by Sawako and Yojiro, who had just ascended the rear staircase.

'Koichi, who's this?'

For some reason, this appeared to be the most urgent question on Yojiro's mind.

'My name is Akimitsu Takagi,' shot back my companion. 'I'm here at your father's request. Now, where did that scream come from? It sounded like it was somewhere on this floor …'

'Yes, it did seem to come from up here,' replied Yojiro. 'Kenkichi—did you hear it?'

The Professor's son, in his pyjamas, had come running out of the room next to Taijiro's and now stood by us, rubbing his eyes.

'It came from Uncle Taijiro's room. I heard a sort of clunk, like something had fallen onto the floor—and then a moment later that scream.'

There was a pause while we all looked at each other. Then Yojiro hurried over to his father's door and began hammering on it.

'Father! Father! Are you okay? What happened?'

But there was no reply. Akimitsu tried the door handle, then kneeled to look through the keyhole.

'Can't see a thing. The key must be in the lock. Young lady, is your father a deep sleeper?'

'No,' replied Sawako. 'In fact, he's so nervous he usually wakes up at the slightest sound.'

'I see. Well, it looks like we'll have to break this door open.'

The family all turned to stare at him.

'Listen, everyone,' continued Akimitsu sharply, 'barely twenty minutes ago, Mr Chizui told me over the phone that he was in imminent danger—that he feared for his life. And now—this scream. Unless there's a flaw in my reasoning, we must entertain the possibility that Mr Chizui is no longer alive. Now, do I have your permission to break this door open?'

'Oh, feel free,' came a low voice. Rintaro was standing half-way down the attic stairs, gazing intently at us.

A hand axe was brought. Akimitsu began swinging away. The axe thudded into the sturdy oak door repeatedly until, finally, it gave way and swung open.

We trooped into the room. First, I checked the lock on the door. It was as Akimitsu had said: the key had been inserted from inside. Second, the windows were all tightly closed, as were the outer iron shutters. Even the pivot windows were now firmly shut.

And, still seated in his armchair by the table, was the corpse of Taijiro Chizui.

His face was contorted in agony, while his eyes seemed riveted on some distant place. There were no noticeable wounds on his body, which was still warm; rigor mortis had not yet set in. There was no murder weapon to be seen.

It was only then that I noticed the strange fragrance pervading the room. A sweet, floral and not unpleasant aroma ... and yet there were no flowers in sight.

'Perfume,' murmured Akimitsu. 'A strong one, too. It must have been sprinkled on the body.'

'Is it suicide?' asked Yojiro, his voice trembling with fear. But Akimitsu did not reply, instead pointing silently to the object that lay by the door.

The *hannya* mask, that bearer of a two-hundred-year-old curse, stared coldly up at us from the floor. Its horns and

47

fangs seemed to quiver with mad delight; I was struck by the impression that it had just drained the lifeblood of its victim.

We stood there silently rooted to the spot—and yet, as if in mockery of our distress, Rintaro extracted a cigarette from the case in his pocket, then clicked his lighter. It seemed even the death of his own father had failed to move him. At the same time I detected, in the deep wrinkles around his mouth and in the depths of his gaze, a sort of fierce challenge to us all.

3

The Chizui Family

After a brief, deathly silence, we regained our composure. The police and a doctor were called, while countless other tasks now demanded the Chizui family's attention.

As for Akimitsu, I imagine he was itching to begin his investigation, and yet he could hardly start interrogating the family before the police arrived. Instead, after ushering everyone into the hallway, he had some chairs brought out from the neighbouring room, sat down on one of them and began rambling about this and that, making repeated references to his beloved detective novels. I found this behaviour quite vexing—and yet the piece of evidence he produced at the end of his lecture floored me completely.

'Now, there's no use trying to rush things, Koichi. We have no authority here anyway. I'm on good terms with the local police chief, Omachi; I'm sure everything will become a lot easier once his officers are here. Though I don't imagine a criminal capable of pulling off a locked-room murder of this sort—right under everyone's nose, no less—will have overlooked anything that would give the game away so early on.

'Based on what you told me about the events of two nights ago, and that panicky phone call from the victim this evening, this murder has been meticulously planned. And yet look at the time: it's barely twenty past nine. If you were going to commit such a shocking crime, why do it now, when almost everyone in the family would still be awake? Why not wait until the middle of the night? I think we learned the answer in that phone call: Taijiro had discovered who the murderer was, and so he had to be silenced for good, before we could get to him.'

'But, Akimitsu, what makes you so sure this was murder? The windows were all closed, the shutters bolted, and the key inserted into the lock from the inside. Even those pivot windows were closed ...'

'Appearances can be deceiving, Koichi. Detective novels are full of these sorts of locked-room murders. I myself am aware of dozens of different methods of executing them. But it's not the method that interests me so much here as *why* the murderer chose the locked-room approach in the first place. That'll be the real crux of the case. Work that out, and it'll probably solve itself.

'Now, I imagine you're thinking Taijiro could have died from natural causes. I suppose next you'll tell me that a man in his fifties, expecting a male visitor, sprinkled perfume all over himself out of vanity? Let me remind you, Koichi: the man was in his pyjamas! And what do you suppose he was doing with that *hannya* mask which he so feared—admiring it? Of course not. No, it seems quite impossible, given the circumstances in which Mr Chizui died, that he did so from natural causes.

'Needless to say, it wasn't suicide either. No visible means, and no note. And what about that panicked tone in his voice on the phone? Would someone who already had his mind set on suicide really preface it with such a terrified plea for help?

'No, we must not be misled by superficial details. We are dealing with a murder—one that appears to have been planned and executed perfectly. There are no visible wounds;

50

Taijiro wasn't shot, stabbed, strangled or bludgeoned to death. In which case, the culprit must have devised some ingenious method of murder—and crucially, one that was guaranteed to work.'

'What about poison?'

'We won't know until we see the autopsy, but I have to say it seems extremely unlikely. Imagine how hard it would be to get someone in such a jittery state to consume any such substance. Not to mention the fact that most poisons produce their effects immediately after being swallowed—and even if there was a delay, it would be very hard to ensure it was of a specific duration.

'Forcing the victim to breathe in poisoned gas would have been similarly difficult, and we would have noticed it when we broke into the room. The murderer may have planned the crime meticulously, but it had to be executed swiftly. There simply wasn't time for anything that complicated.'

'Well, how *do* you suppose he was killed?'

'Let's assume that, as I'm expecting, the autopsy reveals no obvious causes of death. No poison, no internal bleeding—in fact, not a trace of anything. There are several murder methods consistent with this known to forensic science: for example, bludgeoning the head without fracturing the skull, or giving a very sharp blow to the abdomen. Those are both theoretically possible, but in practice any attempt usually results in bone fractures or subcutaneous bleeding. Another technique involves passing a mild electric current through the victim, but that would require their skin to be wet—which doesn't seem to have been the case here …

'When we entered the room, the first thing I did was verify that the key was indeed in the lock. You see, in some locked-room murders the culprit somehow inserts the key only after the door is broken open—but not here. When we were in the hall, you remember I tried turning the handle myself, and even attempted to look through the keyhole: I am certain the key had already been inserted from inside.

'There was no gap at the top or bottom of the door. Both the main windows and the pivot windows were closed. I checked the entire room: there was simply no way that anything—even a thread of string—could have gotten in or out. Of course, the police may find something I missed. But this looks to me, Koichi, like the work of a formidable criminal mastermind.

'Broadly speaking, there are three types of locked-room murders. The first relies on some kind of time differential: for example, after being mortally wounded, the victim voluntarily enters and seals the room, before dying shortly afterwards. The second, probably the most common, is the mechanical type: some kind of contraption inside the room carries out the murder, or a mechanism seals the room after the victim's death. The third relies on an intense psychological shock of some kind—for example, the victim's fear of a ghost.

'So, Koichi, which type do you think we are dealing with? The presence of that mask on the floor strongly hints at the third type, but successfully inflicting a fatal psychological shock within such a strict time frame would be extremely diffi-cult. And what role can the perfume have played? It might have contained poison, but that would show up in the autopsy—and a murderer using such crude methods would be quickly apprehended.

'No, what we should fear above all else is that, instead of using poison or some other chemical, the murderer devised a much more straightforward and reliable method to take the victim's life without leaving the slightest trace. In that case, we will find ourselves at a complete impasse; it may seem that all we can do is throw our hands up in despair. But I believe we still have two important clues: the perfume, and the Noh mask. Understanding their significance will be crucial if we are ever to get to the bottom of all this.

'Now, tell me, Koichi, do you understand this code?'

Akimitsu glanced around to check we were alone before holding up a sheet of paper. I was quite taken aback. It was covered with an array of straight and curved lines, scrawled in pencil.

'What on earth is that? And where did you find it?'

'I found it lying on the stairs when we rushed up them earlier. You may not realize it, but this is actually shorthand. There are various types of shorthand; this happens to be the Nakane method. Now, what do you suppose it says?'

An involuntary shudder ran down my spine. Akimitsu's low voice sounded, to my ears, like a clap of thunder:

'*Hello, is that the Marine Hotel? Could you put me through to Akimitsu Takagi's room? Ah, Mr Takagi? Is Koichi there with you? Could you put him on? Koichi, it's me, Taijiro. Did you meet Mr Takagi? You see, just after you left, something rather ghastly happened. That demon appeared again! I finally learned who was behind the mask … I can't tell you now. Put Mr Takagi on, would you? Ah, Mr Takagi? This is Taijiro Chizui. Sorry for bothering you like this. Did you read my letter? Yes, I'd actually like you to visit tonight, if you could. It's very urgent—do you think you can come over here right this minute? Oh, and don't tell anyone you're coming … As I just told Koichi, I know who was wearing the mask. There isn't a moment to spare … No, I'm sorry, but I can't tell you that over the phone. Please, come at once. I'll be waiting for you.*'

We instinctively looked at each other. It was a transcript of our phone call with Taijiro. Someone had noted down everything he had said in shorthand. The question was: why?

'Who could have written this?' I asked, my voice rising uncontrollably. 'Why would they need a record—wouldn't simply eavesdropping have been enough?'

'That is what I intend to find out.'

'Do you think we can identify the handwriting?'

'Probably not, I'm afraid. Shorthand isn't writing in the conventional sense—it's more like a series of pictures. And identifying the author of a picture is a challenge, even for experts in such things.'

'But why do you suppose they dropped it on the floor? In any case, this seems like a very significant piece of evidence. We'll have to hand it over to the police as soon as they get here.'

'Oh, I'm not planning on showing this to the police.'

It appeared that, once again, Akimitsu was embracing his contrarian nature. Lost for words, I simply stared at him.

'Koichi, perhaps this really was a blunder on the part of the murderer. But what if, instead, it is some kind of challenge? You know—the murderer's way of bragging that even our phone calls aren't as private as we might think? You see, this scrap of paper may be my one and only trump card; as such, I intend to keep it to myself until the last moment. If the police search me and find it, I'll tell them I wrote it myself, in order to record the phone conversation. Match your story to mine, will you? If they ask about the first two sentences, tell them we enquired about them at the hotel reception. I'll need something like this up my sleeve if I'm to prevail against a criminal of this calibre ...'

I listened silently. I knew Akimitsu too well to even try and get a word in edgeways.

Just then, an elderly gentleman with a briefcase appeared at the top of the front stairs, accompanied on either side by

Yojiro and Sawako. This was Doctor Yamamoto, the family physician. He had a heavily receding hairline and a diminutive figure, and must have been in his early sixties.

Akimitsu and I got to our feet and bowed to the doctor, who quickly returned the gesture before disappearing into Taijiro's room. We waited in the hall, practically gritting our teeth with tension. Five minutes, ten minutes … When the doctor finally emerged, his face was tinged with a strange mixture of doubt and fear.

'Did you discover the cause of death?' asked Akimitsu immediately.

'We won't know for sure until the autopsy. But I found no external injuries and no traces of poison. The only cause I can think of is a heart attack brought on by some kind of sudden and overwhelming shock.'

'Did Taijiro have any heart complications?'

'Not at all—in fact, he had a very healthy heart for his age. Could have run a marathon if he'd wanted. I remember him joking about how young he still felt. No other health issues either. It's almost inconceivable for someone like him to suddenly suffer a heart attack like this.'

Akimitsu turned to me with a knowing look.

'See, Koichi? Just as I thought.'

But there was something else bothering me. 'What about the time of death, Doctor?'

He seemed to plunge into thought; when he eventually spoke, it was in a low voice:

'Current medical science is rarely able to estimate the exact hour and minute of a death, especially in a situation like this. The summer heat means it takes an unusually long time for the body to turn cold; rigor mortis has not yet set in. That can take anywhere from one to three hours—or even longer in a hot, humid, sealed room like this one. So it's hard to gain a very precise idea of the timing, really.'

'I imagine Koichi is rather concerned about that particular detail,' came a cold sneer from behind. 'After all, he was the last person to see my father alive. The noose is practically around his neck at this point.'

It was Rintaro. I felt my whole body quiver. If the circumstances had been different, I might well have thrown caution to the wind and leapt at him …

Just then, a gasping voice rose to my defence.

'That's not true! Uncle Taijiro came to my room after Koichi left the house. He asked me: "Did that laughter just now come from in here?" When I told him it hadn't, he replied: "I see. I could have sworn it did …" Then he looked around the room and walked out.'

Kenkichi was barely fourteen years old, and here he was trying desperately to prove my innocence. His large black eyes—a dead ringer for those of his father, the Professor—shimmered with tears. His heart disease had left him with a sickly, waxen complexion. Even just talking at length must have been agony for him. Panting heavily, he leaned against the wall and clutched his chest with both hands.

'What would a child know about such things?' spat Rintaro. 'Stop speaking out of turn.'

'At any rate,' said Akimitsu, 'Taijiro also telephoned us at the Marine Hotel. He told me he was gripped by some terrible fear and asked me to come at once. We hurried here as fast as we could—and were greeted by that scream, and Taijiro's death. Koichi, that scream sounded like Taijiro, didn't it?'

I nodded silently.

'Who *are* you, anyway?' retorted Rintaro. 'Barging into someone else's house, interfering in our family affairs—what gives you the right to speak like this? And how do you even know our father's death was a murder in the first place?'

'My apologies for not introducing myself—Akimitsu Takagi. Koichi and I have been friends since our schooldays. He came to see me earlier this evening regarding Mr Chizui's request for assistance, which I was appraised of in detail both by letter and over the telephone. I therefore consider myself obliged to carry out the deceased's wishes. Fortunately, I am on good terms not only with Chief Inspector Omachi, but various other members of the local police force. Until I've given the police my account of these events, I have no intention of simply disappearing.'

Akimitsu spoke quietly, and yet there was an iron-like determination in his voice which repelled Rintaro's attempts at intimidation. Still, the latter continued his tirade.

'You keep mentioning this phone call of yours, but it's not like you saw him on the television—what proof do you have that it was even my father you were talking to?'

At this accusation, I clenched my fists in surprise. But just then, another witness came unexpectedly to my aid.

'Oh, but I saw Father making the call. I happened to be walking down the hall and saw him in the telephone booth. Koichi is telling the truth. I don't know who my father was calling, but he was definitely on the phone.'

The dignified and sonorous voice belonged to Sawako. She was glaring at Rintaro with a strange fieriness in her eyes. This was particularly unusual behaviour for the meek Sawako, who was normally barely able to look her older brother in the face and always spoke with her eyes cast downwards.

'If you say so,' said Rintaro, before finally falling silent. The pale smoke from his cigarette drifted through our anxious congregation and down the hall. When, presently, he spoke again, it was in a calmer voice.

'My apologies, Mr Takagi. Perhaps I went too far. You see, I have a habit of doubting things until I'm well and truly convinced. I suppose your behaviour may have touched a nerve. Tell me, though—what is it about my father's death that you find so fascinating? Whatever lives must one day die—that is an inescapable fact. Whether that death is from natural causes, suicide or murder—what's the use in moping about it?

'Humans are perfectly happy to take the lives of animals. When a mosquito tries to suck our blood, we swat it without a moment's thought. Why is that? A mosquito needs human blood to survive—such is its fate. But I don't suppose you've ever pitied a mosquito or imagined that its family might grieve its death!

'Humans like to think of themselves as the masters of all creation, but aren't our lives really just as ephemeral as that of the mosquito? Earthquakes, floods, plagues—nature simply has to take one little swing at us for thousands, even millions, of lives to be snuffed out in an instant. And yet we still like to boast that *we*'re the dominant species, the ones who have brought nature to heel. How little we know our place. We'd do well to act a little more humbly, don't you think?

'Just look at the war. Mankind went through the horrors of the First World War and then, before it had even had a chance to finish licking its wounds, decided to embark on another one! Millions of people all trying to slaughter each other—massacres, destruction, genocide. That is the real face of humanity. We are the supreme life form, the only animal with the gift of reason, and that is the grim reality we have chosen for ourselves.

'What, then, is the value of morality? Or, for that matter, laws? They're mere window dressing, I tell you—magic charms for the weak of will. The powerful simply ignore them and create their own reality through their actions. Indeed, their actions *are* the law.

'Say I were to beat someone to death right here and now. I'd be tried for murder, and either spend the rest of my life languishing in a cold prison cell or be whisked off to the gallows. It wouldn't matter if the victim were a complete stranger: my actions would be viewed in the same light.

'And yet imagine I'm sent to war and end up beating a different complete stranger to death with my rifle butt. My actions will be considered those of a hero; I might even get a medal. Why? Because morality is always relative. Today it means one thing; tomorrow another. He who steals a penny is sent to jail; he who steals a country becomes its king. Kill one man and you're a murderer; kill a million and you'll be admired for your patriotism. In morality as in law, the standards are always shifting. Power, on the other hand—*power* is an immutable, physical reality.

'It's the same with our amorous relations. If you think love conquers everything, then think again. Let's say I get down on my knees and profess my love to a woman; she'll laugh in my face and brush me aside like a piece of lint on her dress. Now imagine I make her mine using power instead. I'll be able to ignore, abuse and mistreat her as much as I like, and she'll never leave my side. As long as I'm the one in command, she'll bow down before me and kiss my feet.

'Yes, power is all that prevails in this world—you can prattle on about morals, love or conscience all you like, but without it they mean nothing. Even justice is helpless in the face of it. I despise almost everything, but I will always be drawn to power. Once you have it, anything goes—even murder. That, you see, is my creed.'

Such was the extraordinary lecture that Rintaro insisted on giving while his father lay dead in the neighbouring room. And yet something told me he was not simply letting his tongue get the better of him. In his words I detected a sort of challenge, as if he were casting a gauntlet in my direction.

'I see,' said Akimitsu with a sardonic grin. He had been listening quietly. 'Very interesting. Clearly you have a sharp intellect; or at least a good memory. You see, that's a fine theory, but I'm sure I've heard it somewhere before—practically word for word, too. Let's put your second-hand sophistry to one side; borrowed ideas are of no interest to me. What I really want to know is what made you feel the need to ramble on like this in the first place. Something tells me the *real* you is not this calm lecturer but the person who was getting so worked up a moment ago.'

These fierce words seemed to stun Rintaro into sullen silence.

'Everyone in this family is harbouring secrets—secrets you're all desperate to conceal,' continued Akimitsu. 'Now, I'm not an officer of the law. In fact, I'm no one at all. But if even an amateur like me can tell you're up to something, I can guarantee that a professional detective will see right through you. Still, if you think you can get away with it, be my guests.

'A terrible mystery lurks in this family. Taijiro has already fallen prey to it. And, unless you take a long, hard look at yourselves, I imagine a second crime, even a third, won't be long coming. The next victim could be any one of you. Perhaps then you'll remember the warnings of a man named Akimitsu Takagi. But by then, I fear it'll be too late … Well, I suppose all we can do is wait quietly until the police arrive.'

I could tell Akimitsu was trying to unsettle the Chizui family; these menacing words were an attempt to shatter their sense of superiority. But I couldn't help wondering if his strategy might backfire.

Of the assembled family members, Yojiro was the most visibly perturbed by what Akimitsu had said. Having listened to his older brother with evident irritation, he now stepped forward and said his own piece. His prominent fleshy cheeks contrasted bizarrely with his brother's gaunt, neurotic features. With his small, darting eyes and large hooked nose, he was the spitting image of his father, and when he spoke it was with the same glib tone.

'Bravo, Mr Takagi. I'm very impressed by the way you're handling all this. Still, I'm not sure you quite realize how much an illustrious family like ours would prefer to keep its internal quarrels and secrets to itself. I'm sure my father would tell you as much if he were still with us. At any rate, I wonder if you might not see things from our perspective. As the doctor explained, my father merely appears to have died from some kind of shock-induced heart attack, and there is no material evidence for any of the foul play you're suggesting. So—why don't we keep this all between ourselves for now? The reputation and dignity of the Chizui family hangs in the balance.

'In fact, there'd be a job in it for you, too. We'll do everything we can to assist your investigation, and if you *do* come to the conclusion that our father was murdered, we'll hire you to track down the murderer in a private capacity. You'd operate in strict confidence, without the outside world or police knowing what you're up to, and you wouldn't speak a word about it to anyone—not until you've established who committed the crime. You see, Sawako here isn't even married yet, and my deceased father would hardly have wanted some wild theory to hinder her future prospects. What do you say?'

The pretence was admirable. In all the time I'd been living with the family, this was the first time I'd ever heard Yojiro express any semblance of concern for his sister. Normally, he treated her little better than a maid; I doubted whether she herself had ever heard him weigh in on her marriage prospects like this.

Akimitsu puffed calmly on his cigarette as he listened, the faintest of smiles playing around his lips.

'Of course, I am not here to stir things up unnecessarily. But I'm also not the type to turn a blind eye where justice is concerned. I'm afraid I don't subscribe to Rintaro's views on the unconditional glorification of power or the irrelevance of morality: if Mr Chizui was indeed murdered, I refuse to allow his killer to roam free.

'At the same time, my purpose is not to meddle in the affairs of others or inconvenience the innocent. I promise to do my utmost to keep these matters in confidence and avoid any unnecessary disclosure to the public. However, given the fate that has today befallen Mr Chizui—the man who requested my services in the first place—I cannot yield an inch towards the murderer. And I certainly won't stand and watch as the blood of a second or third victim is spilled. So if I am to do as you request, I must ask one condition in return.'

Nobody moved a muscle. The members of the family each seemed to be grappling with their own secret fears.

'And what might that be?' asked Yojiro in a reedy voice. 'If it's money you'd like, I'm sure we can accommodate you …'

'Oh, I don't need money. No, my condition is simply this: that you all cooperate fully in helping me get to the bottom of this murder.'

With this assertion, he stared at the faces of those assembled. Other than Rintaro, nobody met his gaze. Yojiro and Sawako glanced away in apparent trepidation, while Kenkichi hung his head and gave a painful-sounding cough.

'You really are a peculiar lot, aren't you? The father of the family has just been murdered, and yet nobody seems the least bit upset, or even eager to find out who did it! Perhaps you all already know, and you're trying to cover it up? Or is it that you agree with Rintaro that the powerful should be allowed to get away with murder? Or are you simply afraid of what will happen to anyone who dares to speak out? Well, I suppose the precise reasons don't matter. Your actions from now on will determine whether I become your enemy or your ally. I suggest you think long and hard about them.'

Such was Akimitsu's haughty challenge to the family. For a while, nobody said a word.

Eventually, Yojiro raised a hand as if to speak. But just as he did so, a raspy voice issued from the other end of the hallway. There was something uncanny, almost demonic, about it.

'Enough with this *racket*! What are you all blabbering on about?'

Cane in hand, the aged Sonoe Chizui, mother of the deceased, appeared in the hallway. Her mild palsy prevented her from moving the right side of her body freely, but she was still just about able to walk. Doctor Yamamoto had recommended she remain in bed as much as possible, but she had always had a reputation as a strong-willed madam and remained as intractable as ever in her old age. Deep wrinkles lined the saggy flesh of her oval face, once surely the subject of much adulation; her two eyes retained a piercing gleam, like the smouldering embers of a once-blazing fire.

'Well, what's going on? And who are *you*?' she asked, glaring suspiciously at Akimitsu.

'My apologies, madam. My name is Akimitsu Takagi. I regret to inform you that Taijiro was found dead in his room this evening. What's more, he may have been murdered.'

At this the old woman teetered and lost her balance. Her cane clattered to the floor. Sawako rushed to her side to support her, while Yojiro bent down for the cane and returned it to her. Rintaro merely looked on in silence, without lifting a finger to help.

'Taijiro? Murdered? And who are you accusing of murdering him?'

'I can't say as yet. The doctor says it was a heart attack brought on by an extreme shock of some kind. We found that family heirloom of yours, the Noh mask, lying near his body.'

'What! The mask?'

Her face contorted with shock. For a moment she remained speechless, though a strange sound, somewhere between a growl and a groan, seemed to issue from her throat.

'It's the curse of the mask! I warned you all, didn't I? I told you: get that mask out of this house! Now, after two hundred years, the curse of Gennojo Hosho has finally returned!'

'My dear madam, I'm afraid a supernatural explanation like that doesn't hold much water these days. We live in an age of science; we cannot simply explain things away with ghost stories or the idea that some ancient curse might be wreaking its vengeance. Do you have any kind of physical evidence for this claim of yours?'

'Science, eh? What would *you* know about science? Soichiro was one of the country's leading scientists, and even he was unable to foresee or prevent his own death! I tell you, this world of ours is full of secrets your science or philosophy will never understand. Now, how about you stop poking your nose in our affairs … Oh, and I wouldn't dismiss this as an old lady's rambling if I were you! No matter how many years go by, a grudge is a grudge. Yes—tonight, the curse has reared its head once again …'

Her low murmuring seemed to emanate from the very depths of hell. Coming face to face with Taijiro's corpse had been a daunting experience—and yet there are times when confronting a living person can be an even more terrifying prospect. This felt like one such moment. I was shaking from head to toe, as if I had been drenched with icy water.

But it was not only Sonoe's words that made us quiver with fear. There was more horror to come. A maid came hurrying up the back stairs, her face pale as she broke the silence.

'Miss Sawako, the undertaker's here. Apparently someone phoned him earlier—said sorry to bother him this late at night, but it was urgent and he'd be paid extra for the trouble. He says he came over here as fast as he could.'

We all looked at each other. Who could have made the call? And what on earth could this mean?

'Well, who was it?' asked Rintaro, his sharp voice piercing the graveyard-like hush that had descended in the hallway. 'Which one of you could *possibly* have thought to call the undertaker?'

Nobody replied, though a vague murmuring sprang up among the family, creating a sort of hum not unlike that of a swarm of tiny insects. Akimitsu appeared to be quietly studying the faces of everyone present.

He turned to Sonoe. 'Madam, it appears the mask was not content with simply putting a deadly curse on Taijiro. I suppose ghosts are more considerate these days, and even go to the trouble of telephoning the undertaker on our behalf?'

By now his sarcasm had exceeded the limits of what the members of the Chizui family could tolerate. A stream of invective began to issue from the mouths of Rintaro and Yojiro; I did not have the courage to stop them. The din that had erupted seemed to me like the goings-on of a distant country. But the commotion did not last long. For what felt like the tenth time that evening, everyone froze as the maid came running up the front stairs, her words ringing sharply in our ears.

'Ladies and gentlemen—the police are here!'

4

The Mirage

(Koichi Yanagi's journal, continued)

'Everyone, please retire to your rooms for now. We'll need to interview you all individually in a moment. Until then, try to get some rest.'

The young officer in charge of the investigation, Inspector Yoshino, gave his instructions quietly and politely. With an unexplained death in the illustrious Chizui family, and uncertainty hovering over whether murder or natural causes were to blame, he had clearly concluded that this was the only way to proceed.

'Koichi, I'm scared,' said Kenkichi, clinging fiercely to my hand. 'Will you stay with me?'

His fear was only natural given the circumstances. I glanced at Inspector Yoshino, who gave a brief, silent nod of approval. Glad to finally leave the hallway, I followed Kenkichi into the room he shared with Hisako.

'I'll come with you,' said Akimitsu from behind us. He seemed similarly relieved. He had managed to keep the various members of the Chizui family, none of whom he seemed to trust, from disturbing the scene of the crime; just handing it over to the police must have been a considerable weight off his mind.

Like most of the mansions dotted along the Miura peninsula, the Chizui residence was built entirely in the Western style. The first floor was divided up into six large bedrooms. Taijiro's room, where the murder had occurred, occupied one end of the north side of the hallway. Next was Kenkichi and Hisako's, where we now sat, and after that was the bedroom shared by Sawako and Sonoe. On the other side of the hallway, the first room was the unoccupied one where the Noh mask was kept, the second Rintaro's, and the third Yojiro's. Each of the rooms was the size of twelve tatami mats—about twenty square metres—and equipped with Western-style beds and furniture.

After all the tension in the hallway, we could finally breathe again. The three of us collapsed into chairs and wiped the sweat from our foreheads. Of course, this wasn't the end of the matter; we would still have to undergo questioning by the police. And yet my anxiety about that intimidating prospect was accompanied by the calm feeling that the worst was already out of the way. All the agitation and excitement of a few moments ago had been quite draining—for me as much as anyone else.

The maid arrived with some chilled black tea. My throat was completely parched, though I had barely noticed until now. I drained the glass in one go. During the war, I had experienced terrible thirst over and over; in the jungles of Burma, where our water filters did practically nothing, I had smacked my lips countless times at the mere sight of muddy swamp water. And yet I shall never forget the taste of that glass of black tea. It felt somehow as though I were dissolving, from head to toe, into some other world.

'Do you like mountain climbing, Kenkichi?' asked Akimitsu in a low voice. His eyes were fixed on the ice axe hanging in one corner of the room.

'That's not mine. My sister used to go climbing—before she became ill, that is.'

I had seen the axe before. When she was still a schoolgirl, I had accompanied her on a summer climbing expedition to the northern Japanese Alps, where she had demonstrated admirable bravery and skill. I could still recall the sight of her beautiful face as she stood on the summit of Mount Yari, wisps of fog streaming wildly past, her jet-black hair fluttering in the wind as she gazed across a sea of clouds. The image came to me as clearly as if it had been yesterday, and yet it was really no more than the fragment of a dream—one that would never be real again. Though her beauty had not faded, there was something about the sight of the now-crazed Hisako lying there on her bed, having slept right through this eventful summer evening, that brought a tear to my eye.

'Ah,' said Akimitsu, nodding slowly. 'Your sister's, eh?' The gentle gaze he directed at Hisako's sleeping face seemed filled with sympathy.

'Koichi,' came a voice from the hall. 'Inspector Yoshino will see you now.' The time had come. I steeled myself, just as I had whenever the enemy launched a sudden assault at the front. A nasty chill crept through my entire body.

'Relax, you'll be fine,' said Akimitsu, patting me reassuringly on the shoulder. 'I'll be waiting here.'

Kenkichi looked up at me nervously as I left the room. I slowly made my way downstairs and knocked on the door of the reception room.

'Please, come in.'

Inspector Yoshino was sitting in the room, together with several other police officers. Among them I caught sight of Mr Ishikari. Following our sighting of the masked figure in the window, he'd taken a week's leave and was staying at a local inn; presumably the police had notified him of the murder and he'd decided to come along. However, tonight he was not the fatherly figure I knew personally, but an impartial representative of the law.

'Ah, Koichi. Take a seat.'

I slowly sat down in front of Mr Ishikari. After confirming my name, age and date of birth, Inspector Yoshino leaned forward and began the questioning.

'So, what time was it when you left Taijiro's room?'

'Exactly twenty past eight.'

'I see. And when did you discover the body?'

'Almost twenty past nine, I think. Maybe seventeen or eighteen minutes past.'

'In other words, Taijiro's death must have occurred within that window of roughly one hour. But tell me—what made you think it was murder? There were no visible wounds or signs of poisoning, and the room was completely sealed from the inside, wasn't it?'

'Akimitsu Takagi—the friend who came here with me—took one look at the body and concluded it was murder. He told us to phone the police immediately. The family were in quite a state of shock, so I suppose they didn't think too deeply about it and simply did as he said.

'But I have to say I agree with him. I know there's no hard evidence in the form of external injuries to the body, but you have to realize that the atmosphere in this house was unbearably tense prior to Taijiro's death. Under those circumstances, I find it hard to believe he could have simply died from natural causes. I see we are fortunate enough to be joined by Mr Ishikari. Two nights ago, when he accompanied me back to the house, we saw someone wearing the mask staring out of one of the upstairs windows. Of course, that seemed very odd, so we went inside and asked Taijiro to show us the room in question. But by then, the mask was already back in its case—and

70

the only person in the room was Hisako, who was hunched over the piano.

'Tonight, Taijiro seemed terribly anxious about something, and asked me if I knew any private detectives. When I recommended Akimitsu, he immediately wrote a letter requesting his assistance. I took the letter to Akimitsu at his hotel, and while we were discussing the situation, Taijiro called on the telephone. He was in a terrible panic, and said he knew who'd been wearing the mask. We hurried to the house, and as we were ringing the doorbell, we heard a scream. We broke Taijiro's door open and found his body—and, lying on the floor nearby, that mask.

'I don't think any of that can be explained away as some bizarre coincidence, or the work of some supernatural force. I am convinced this was a vicious murder. For the sake of justice, and Taijiro's departed spirit, I sincerely hope the truth comes to light as soon as possible.'

'Koichi's right,' Mr Ishikari chimed in assertively. 'This was a meticulously plotted murder—there's no doubt about it. Once I'd seen that mask in the window, I couldn't shake the feeling that something sinister was going to happen in this house.'

'Mr Yanagi,' continued Yoshino, 'when you discovered the body at around twenty past nine, had anything about the room changed during the preceding hour?'

'When I left the room, I'm almost certain the pivot windows were still open. But by the time we found Taijiro's body, even those had been closed. Also, the Noh mask wasn't lying on the floor when I left.'

'I see. Taijiro must really have been on edge, to have closed and shuttered the windows like that. The upstairs windows of a mansion like this are so high up it would be practically impossible for anyone to get in or out of them. What on earth could he have been so afraid of?'

'That mask, perhaps?'

'I suppose—after all, it *was* found lying near the corpse ... Now, this is an important question. After you left the house, did anyone else see the victim while he was still alive?'

'When we were talking in the hallway just now, Kenkichi mentioned that after I left the house, Taijiro came into his room to ask him something. Then, later on, it seems Sawako saw him making a phone call.'

Kenkichi speaking out on my behalf had been one thing, but the testimony of Sawako was an additional, unexpected lifeline.

'I'll follow that up with those two, then. As long as their stories check out, you'll have yourself an alibi, and there'll be nothing for you to worry about. Incidentally, do you have any ideas as to who might be behind this crime?'

'I don't have any firm suspicions yet. But if I think of any potential leads, I'll be sure to let you know.'

I stood and bowed. But as I left the room, I heard Mr Ishikari murmur to the others in the room:

'Gentlemen, if tonight's murder was a Noh play, it was quite a twist on the standard performance. The question is: what prop did the demon carry onto the stage?'

There was a long history of making adjustments to the orthodox version of Noh plays, whether that meant varying the dances, music, props or masks. Not content to simply adhere to a play's established form, actors would add their own creative variations—or, in some cases, simply make a mistake that was then retained in performance because of the unexpected effect it produced—and these variations would be incorporated into an alternative version of the play. What might Mr Ishikari have meant by comparing the murder to one of these variations? Had he already grasped the truth behind the affair? And what was the significance of this 'prop' he was referring to?

Back in Kenkichi and Hisako's room, I found Akimitsu sitting by a lamp, thumbing the pages of a book.

'That all went smoothly, then?'

'Oh, yes—though it's hard not to get a little worked up in a situation like that. What's that you're reading?'

'Hisako's diary. Kenkichi, tell me—when did your sister become … ill?'

'Five years ago.'

'Ah—that explains why her diary stops at that point. Still, it's a little odd how some of the sections from ten years ago have been torn out. Could that period hold some special meaning, I wonder? She would have been seventeen or eighteen at the time … And that's not all. Some pages appear to have been torn from the diary from seven years ago, too. Who could have done a thing like that, I wonder … Kenkichi, when did you and your sister start living with your uncle?'

'I think it was soon after my father's death, when my mother was sent to the asylum. I was very little at the time, though, so I don't remember much from those days.'

'I see. Now, Koichi, what do you make of this poem?'

Near the end of the diary was a poem, traced in Hisako's beautiful handwriting. Akimitsu began to read it in a low voice.

The Mirage

In deepest autumn, the pale moon rises over the bounding main.
Drawn by a mysterious force, I make for the shore alone.

Cold, desolate dunes, like the remains of sea beasts, stretch into the distance;
The red pines cast their shadows, their trunks wet with dew.

73

The faint scent of flowers distracts me from the sky above;
My heart is pierced by an empty gust of wind.

The midnight air trembles with a flute-like melody,
Now faint and fleeting, now lively and proud;

All of a sudden, I see the waxen hands of a young maiden,
Clutching two shells from which she blows her beautiful
    tune,

Her pale crimson garments dampened and darkened by the
    sea,
Her chest glowing with luminous algae from the deep,

What deep and insurmountable sorrow lurks, I wonder,
Behind that smiling face, those round black eyes?

The shells she holds once lay in the depths,
Old legends say they can summon a mirage:

If, under an autumn moon, you blow the secret melody,
Those once lost will return for a time.

Three years ago, my lover perished in this sea,
Torn from this world by a merciless storm;

The next dawn, his body returned to this beach,
His hand still gripping one of these red shells.

After much grieving, I tried to follow him to the grave,
Yet, saved by a fishing boat, was forced back to this world.

Now, using the shell he brought back from those depths,
I call out to him through the night, yearning to hear that voice
   again.

Behold, my lover has awakened from his sleep;
He walks towards me through the distant waves.

The mist gathers, the wind rises, the shorebirds cry out in vain;
When I glance up again, I see nothing but the surging sea.

The maiden, too, has disappeared from view,
And all that remains, on those fog-shrouded dunes, are the two
   red shells.

'... Two red shells, eh? Well, it's a little old-fashioned, but the romanticism is quite charming,' murmured Akimitsu to no one in particular. 'I have to say, these days I find classical poetry like this much more appealing than anything written in the modern style.'

Who could have guessed at the terrifying meaning lurking in the poem? Akimitsu, for one, certainly didn't seem to have grasped its secrets.

The night wore on, fearful and agitated. I had no way of knowing what sort of questioning the Chizui family underwent, but it seems Akimitsu visited Chief Inspector Omachi and Inspector Yoshino later on and persuaded them to reveal what they'd learned. The following afternoon, I visited his room at the Marine Hotel, where he filled me in on their progress.

If the murder were to be solved, it would be crucial to establish what each member of the family had done between twenty past eight and twenty past nine that evening. However, none of their individual testimonies seemed to tally with each other, making it impossible to establish a reliable timeline of events.

Rintaro claimed that he had been developing photos in the room directly above the scene of the crime—a storage room in the attic that had been converted into a darkroom. Knowing Rintaro, it seemed likely that these photos were of a dubious nature; in any case, he claimed to have heard nothing unusual from below.

The only family members on the first floor had been Kenkichi and Hisako, who were both in their room, and the elderly Sonoe, bedridden in her own room. Yojiro and Sawako had been in the study downstairs, but at around ten minutes to nine, Sawako had left Yojiro on his own; she claimed to have gone out to the gazebo in the garden, where she sat gazing pensively at the ocean until, hearing the scream from upstairs, she rushed into the house via the rear entrance.

None of the family members had a solid alibi; at the same time, there was no clear evidence that any of them had done anything particularly suspicious. The autopsy was still ongoing, but the results so far seemed to confirm what Doctor Yamamoto had said: no sign of poisoning, and no visible injuries. Despite extensive investigation, the cause of death was still unclear. Heart failure due to extreme shock seemed to be the only possible explanation.

No fingerprints had been found on the Noh mask, and nor was it clear what role it could have played in the crime. One thing that had particularly caught the attention of the police was a lump of lead that had been attached to the mask's right horn, perhaps in order to increase its weight. Still, it hardly seemed likely that the mask had been used to bludgeon the victim.

At this point, Akimitsu launched into one of his character-istic bursts of pedantry.

'Now, everyone keeps calling it a *hannya* mask, but technically speaking, that's not quite the right term. You see, there are three types of demon masks in Noh: the *namanari*, the *hannya* and the *jya*. They were designed to express the demon's vindictiveness and jealousy, with the extent of such feelings symbolized by the length of the horns. The *hannya* has longer horns than a *namanari*, but those of a *jya* are longer still. I believe the mask in question to be of the *jya* type. As for its year of production, this can be deduced from the nostrils. Older masks like this one tend to have oval-shaped nostrils, similar to those of humans, whereas those from around the seventeenth century onwards simply feature two round apertures, like they've simply been pierced with a skewer. Of course, a detail that small has no direct bearing on the performance of a play, but still—that sort of corner-cutting, presumably introduced to cut down on labour, seems emblematic of the way in which Noh mask craftsmanship fell into decline after the golden age of the fourteenth and fifteenth centuries.'

'Mr Ishikari has already schooled me in the finer points of Noh, Akimitsu. What does any of this have to do with the case at hand?'

'All in due time, Koichi! In a situation like this, the most important thing is not to rush. This mask appears, at the very least, to be a significant clue, and it would certainly be wise to brush up on our knowledge of its background. Even the most trivial-seeming details, when assembled in the correct manner, can prove vital.'

'If you say so … Anyway, have the police formally decided to treat this as a murder investigation?'

'Of course they have! I suppose you haven't heard the details of that phone call to the undertakers? Apparently, the caller ordered not one, but three coffins. The killer must be planning another two murders, Koichi. Taijiro's death was just the opening act.

'Still, I believe I succeeded in giving the members of the Chizui family a suitable jolt last night. I didn't expect anyone to come forward immediately, what with all the excitement—but I'm sure they'll start talking soon.'

Just then, a bellboy knocked on the door.

'Sir, you have a visitor. A Mr Yojiro Chizui.'

'You see?' said Akimitsu, smiling at me ironically over his shoulder.

It was two o'clock on a hot summer afternoon, and outside the large window of the hotel room, an enormous column of white cloud was gathering in the middle of an otherwise clear blue sky. Below, waves glittered and danced in the sunshine. And yet at that moment, a cold chill was creeping through my body. The murderer was planning a total of three murders, and had signalled as much. The sign of death hung over the entire Chizui family—including the man who had just been announced.

As Yojiro entered the room, I saw none of the previous night's agitation on his face. In its place was the extreme wariness of a natural coward.

'Mr Takagi, my apologies for last night. What with our father passing away in such strange circumstances, I'm afraid we all got a little worked up. Please forgive me if I overstepped the mark.'

'Not in the slightest. Please, take a seat. What brings you here today?'

'I need your help.'

'Mr Chizui, as I told you yesterday, I am merely a private citizen. I consider myself impartial in this matter. In exchange for my assistance, are you willing to confide in me fully?'

A strange sweat had formed on Yojiro's brow, and clearly not just from the heat. From somewhere in the distance came the dull roll of thunder, and yet, even with the window wide open, the air in the room was deathly still.

Akimitsu picked up his pencil and began scrawling something on a sheet of paper on the desk. Peering closer, I was startled to see that he had written in shorthand:

YOJIRO CHIZUI IS THE MURDERER

But nothing in Yojiro's expression changed. Even when he glanced directly at the scribbled note, he continued puffing on his cigarette.

Akimitsu, who appeared to have been carefully watching for Yojiro's reaction, now put his pencil down as if in disappointment.

'Well then, what is it you'd like to tell me?'

'Mr Takagi, when you said last night that my father might have been murdered, I scoffed at the idea. But after giving the matter some thought, I can see you might be onto something after all. Indeed, I think I know what the motive was.'

'Do you now? And what might that be?'

'Money. The hidden motive for this murder is none other than the Chizui family fortune.'

'But surely you and your siblings are the ones who stand to benefit from your father's death in that regard? Or did he leave some kind of unusual will?'

'I'm not talking about the family's public fortune. There is another legacy. No one knows exactly where it is, but it certainly exists—and it has a value of tens of millions of yen.

'As you know, my uncle, Soichiro, passed away ten years ago. Shortly afterwards, his wife went mad, and seeing as Kenkichi and Hisako were both still children, my father became the executor of the estate. Now, ours is an illustrious family, with a lineage that dates back to before the Meiji period. We were all convinced that by now the family fortune would be worth tens, if not hundreds, of millions of yen. But when my uncle died, he left behind practically nothing apart from our Tokyo residence and this country retreat. And yet he'd never been one to waste money on drink or women, and nor did he have any business ventures to speak of. It seems quite impossible that he could have squandered the entire fortune.

'However, we do know that before his death, my uncle was concerned about Japan's prospects in the war. There are indications that, anticipating a massive wave of inflation, he decided to convert the entire family fortune into a highly valuable object of some kind. As for what that object might have been, or where he could have hidden it, we simply have no idea. We've spent the past decade searching all over for it—combing every nook and cranny of both the Tokyo house and our mansion here. Not for our own sake, you understand—we simply felt we had to do what was right for Hisako and Kenkichi. At any rate, I believe the whereabouts of the fortune must be the key to this entire affair.'

'I see,' said Akimitsu, his eyes gleaming with barely contained joy at this new revelation about the family. 'But how would that constitute a motive? Couldn't the murderer simply have gone after the fortune itself? It seems your uncle knew no more than anyone else about its whereabouts. What would killing him achieve?'

'Quite a lot, actually. If you look at the Professor's line of the family, both his wife and Hisako have gone mad, while Kenkichi's heart disease means he won't be with us much longer. If the fortune *is* discovered, it'll end up in my branch of the family instead. And with my father dead, my siblings and I are the ones who stand to profit.'

'Mr Chizui, are you saying it must have been your brother or sister who committed the crime?'

'Oh, not necessarily. Simply, I believe the murderer has somehow discovered the whereabouts of the hidden fortune. Now if it was something relatively light and portable—a jewel, say—there might have been no need to go as far as murder. But instead it must be something difficult to move, leaving the murderer with no option but to commit their horrible crime. Mr Takagi, this is where I need your help. I heard about those three coffins being ordered by telephone; it no longer seems plausible that my father's death was a suicide, or that he died from natural causes. Now, my father, my brother, my sister and myself makes four people. Do you see? If one of us is the killer, the other three must be the intended victims! I don't want to die a miserable death, Mr Takagi—and yet if last night is anything to go by, we are dealing with a truly ingenious and audacious criminal. Who's to say I won't soon follow my father into the grave?

'Please—help me. I'm obliged to remain at the mansion while the investigation into my father's death continues. Help me find the hidden treasure. I'll be sure to reward you handsomely. If we can just discover its location, I'm sure we'll learn the killer's identity in the process, and we'll be able to put a stop to this bloodshed.'

Akimitsu had closed his eyes. It almost looked as though he'd fallen asleep, although he was still puffing on the pipe he always carried, creating a thick cloud of pale smoke. I knew this to be a habit of his whenever something had truly seized his interest; to me, at least, it was evident that he was excited and enthused in equal measure. But was he really capable of unearthing the secrets of the Chizui family? My honest opinion was that, in all likelihood, he wasn't.

'Very well. I'll help you as best I can. But in order to do so, I'll need to be given free rein at the house. Will that be possible?'

'Certainly. Search wherever you please.'

'What about your brother? Won't he mind?'

'Rintaro isn't too concerned about these sorts of material worries. As long as you don't go prying in his room, I'm sure he won't get in your way.'

'Then I'll drop by the mansion soon—perhaps tomorrow. In the meantime, don't let your guard down!'

Yojiro rose to leave. Akimitsu showed him out of the room, then turned back to me with an eager look on his face.

'Well, talk about showing your true colours! Still, we're not quite there yet. This hidden treasure shouldn't be too difficult to find, but I reckon Yojiro is hiding another, darker secret. I'm sure we'll know what that is before long, but at any rate, we've made our first inroads into the mystery of the Chizui family. The important thing now is that we seize this opportunity to find out what *we* really want to know.

'The hidden treasure is of no interest to us. But Yojiro must have had a reason for deliberately telling me about it. No doubt he's hoping to distract my attention from elsewhere and keep me from discovering the real secret. At the same time, if I do manage to track down the treasure, I imagine he'll want to claim it all for himself. Yes, our man wants to have his cake and eat it. Never mind—I'm sure I can turn this situation to our advantage. Come on, let's go. We'll use his request as an excuse to do some more snooping around the mansion.'

Just as he got to his feet, there was another knock at the door. It was the bellboy again.

'Mr Takagi, a lady named Sawako Chizui is here to see you.'

I gave an involuntary start. Of course, I had realized by now that Sawako must have some connection in the case. But what could be her purpose in visiting Akimitsu now? I wanted to hear what she had to say; at the same time, I was reluctant to face her after our encounter the previous day.

Akimitsu must have noticed my consternation, because he turned and quietly indicated the balcony. I dashed out and hid behind one of the shutters.

'Thank you for coming,' came Akimitsu's low, calm voice. 'Please take a seat. Awfully hot today, isn't it?'

'I'm sorry to bother you,' replied Sawako softly. 'Oh … Koichi isn't here, then?'

'He just left. You didn't see him on the way?'

'No, I didn't. He must have stopped somewhere, I suppose … Anyway, Mr Takagi, I must apologize for last night. I'm quite furious at my brothers for treating you like that. That's all I came to say, really, but I suppose I'd also like to ask for your help. Do you have any ideas as to who might be behind my father's murder?'

'Oh, not particularly …'

There was a strange, prolonged silence. Eventually, it was broken by a high-pitched shriek from Sawako.

'Mr Takagi! But … you … why would you write a thing like …'

'Ah, so you *can* read shorthand! I wrote "Sawako Chizui is the murderer" on this piece of paper, and look—you've jumped up and gone pale in the face! You see, I know for a fact that the murderer also knows shorthand. When Koichi and I were talking in this room yesterday evening, your father telephoned me. Someone recorded everything he said in shorthand, and I found the resulting transcript lying on the stairs. Now, Sawako, you mentioned that you happened to pass down the hall while your father was on the phone and spot him through the glass door of the phone booth. And yet the only place where anyone could eavesdrop on the telephone booth would be that very hallway.

'Also, everything your father said is recorded on that piece of paper—not one word has been omitted from the transcript. If it had been someone else listening in, they'd have been obliged to hide somewhere while you walked past, and there would be a corresponding gap in the transcript. And yet—no gap! In other words, the only person who could have recorded that conversation in shorthand is you, Sawako.

'Of course, I'm not saying you are the murderer. But I reckon you at least know their name. So, how about coming clean? Or should I phone the police and tell them about my little discovery?'

My fists were clenched with tension. When he started grilling someone like this, Akimitsu was like a man possessed. But when Sawako replied, it was in a surprisingly calm voice.

'Mr Takagi, it appears I overestimated you. Yes, I'm familiar with the Nakane method. But learning shorthand is not like picking up a foreign language; anyone of reasonable intelligence can learn to read it within a couple of days, and write it within a fortnight or so. So what makes you so sure I'm the only one in the family who knows it?

'As for that phone call, you seem to have assumed that when I passed my father in the phone booth, it was you he was speaking to. But what if he was talking to someone else? Isn't it possible that it was only *after* I had passed by that someone else appeared and recorded that particular conversation in shorthand? Have you made enquiries with the telephone exchange?'

This rebuttal seemed to catch Akimitsu off guard. But he was not ready to admit defeat.

'Well, let me ask you this: why were you walking past the telephone booth in the first place? If you were making your way from the study to the garden, as you claimed, surely you could have just used the back door? Why go all the way to the front one?'

'As it happens, I'd left my knitting on the piano upstairs, and I went up the front stairs to retrieve it.'

'Oh! You didn't mention *that* to the police, did you? So you actually went into the spare room at that time?'

'Yes. I just didn't think it was worth mentioning.'

'Miss Sawako, a detail *you* consider irrelevant may well be crucial in the eyes of an investigator. Tell me, was the Noh mask still in its case?'

'No. The case was open, and the mask was gone.'

'And do you remember what time that was?'

'A little before nine o'clock.'

'What did you do next?'

'I retrieved my knitting, then I went down the back stairs and out of the rear entrance. I sat in the gazebo in the garden. Then I heard that scream, and rushed back into the house.'

'You can see your father's window from the gazebo, can't you? You didn't notice anything unusual?'

'Well, the shutters were closed.'

'Of course. What about the pivot windows?'

'I believe they were closed too. I remember looking up at them.'

'While you were sitting there, did anything unusual happen?'

'No, I didn't notice anything out of the ordinary—until the scream, that is ...'

'I see. Well, Miss Sawako, what was it you wanted to tell me, anyway?'

I heard Sawako get to her feet.

'Mr Takagi, I'm afraid you don't seem to understand women very well. Yes, I came here to ask you something, but you have taken my dignity and dashed it to pieces with your little interrogation. I don't feel like telling you much about anything any more. I'll be leaving now.'

There was the sound of the door opening and then closing. When I emerged from behind the shutter, Akimitsu was alone, smiling bitterly as he puffed on his pipe.

'Well, Koichi, that didn't go very well—as I'm sure you heard.'

'But her idea of investigating the phone calls—that's something, isn't it? In a rural area like this, it shouldn't be too hard to get that sort of information from the local telephone exchange. Don't you think we should find out what phone calls were made from the house last night?'

For once, Akimitsu did as I suggested. He dialled a number and was soon connected to the police, whom he asked to make the necessary enquiries at the telephone exchange.

Ten, twenty, thirty minutes went by in the twinkle of an eye. An hour later, the telephone bell rang furiously—and when Akimitsu replaced the receiver and turned to me, his voice was just as wild with excitement.

'Someone made a long-distance call from the Chizui residence last night—to the Oka Asylum in Tokyo. On top of that, the call was made shortly before nine o'clock—just after the calls to the hotel and the undertaker.'

5

Second Act

We made our way back to the Chizui mansion. Leaden, low-hanging thunderclouds cast an ominous shroud over the dark grey structure. Last night, this house had been the scene of the first murder—and a second and third had already been foretold. Now, whenever I walked through its door, I felt a violent tremor of fear.

We found Yojiro puffing restlessly on a cigarette in his room. Judging by the enormous pile of cigarette butts balanced precariously on his ashtray, he was in quite an agitated mood.

'Please, take a seat,' he said, gesturing to two chairs. 'I thought you weren't coming until tomorrow.'

'Yes, we had a little time on our hands, so we thought it best to come over right away. Has anything unusual happened since we spoke?'

'Well, Mr Takagi, ghosts only come out at night, don't they?'

'I'm glad you haven't lost your sense of humour. Now, I'd like to have a look around the house, if you wouldn't mind?'

'You have the run of the place. Just don't go into anyone's bedroom without permission, please.'

'I'd like to see Professor Chizui's laboratory and study, as well as the darkroom in the attic.'

'Why's that?'

'All in good time. You see, that Noh mask had a lump of lead fixed to its right horn, and I'm curious as to why. Lead isn't exactly a common household item, but I hear this mansion is equipped with a laboratory that the Professor used for his experiments. I believe Koichi has been using it to produce sweeteners for your family. Anyway, I'd like to have a look in there—do you keep it locked?'

'We used to. But with Koichi working there every day, we've started leaving it open.'

'I see. So anyone could just wander in …'

The three of us filed out of the room and down the stairs. The laboratory was a spacious windowed room on the side of the mansion that faced the sea. What with the events of the previous evening, I hadn't been in there today, but as a scientist I always found the sharp chemical odour that filled the room quite nostalgic. As a student, I'd once been confined to bed for a month with illness. Upon finally returning to the university laboratory, what I'd found most comforting had been the familiar rotten-egg smell of hydrogen sulphide that assaulted my nostrils.

For a private laboratory, the room was more than adequately equipped. There was no gas supply, but with the help of an oil burner and an electric stove, I'd been able to produce the saccharin and dulcin the family required.

'Koichi, when were you last in here?'

'Yesterday. I left when I finished my work for the day, at around six in the evening.'

'Those chemicals on the shelf. Is anything missing?'

I studied the shelf. After a month of using them, I had become quite familiar with the stock of chemicals and their usual arrangement. Two bottles were absent from their places.

'The sulphuric acid and the zinc are both missing.'

'Interesting. I know sulphuric acid is highly corrosive, but I don't see what role it could have played in the murder. And what on earth could the zinc be used for? Any ideas, Koichi?'

Akimitsu appeared well and truly perplexed. This was my time to shine.

'Sulphuric acid can be combined with zinc to produce hydrogen. Your average schoolboy knows that, Akimitsu ...'

'Steady, now! You might take me for an idiot, but I'll have you remember I'm a qualified engineer. I know it produces hydrogen—but that's not poisonous, is it? Could it have triggered the heart attack somehow, I wonder?'

'Out of the question. Of course, you could die from breathing nothing but hydrogen, but that would simply be a death by suffocation—not a heart attack. In any case, it would be quite tricky to administer a supply of pure hydrogen to someone in the first place.'

'I suppose you're right. If it were hydrogen cyanide or hydrogen arsenide we were talking about, you could kill someone by getting them to inhale the gas, but not with hydrogen alone ... So why steal the zinc and sulphuric acid? Are any other substances missing—a poison of some kind, perhaps?'

'No, nothing else.'

'Right. What about the lead—where's that kept?'

'Here.' I pulled down a large glass jar from the shelf above the chemical rack and handed it to Akimitsu. He removed the block of lead from the jar and studied it.

'Look—someone has cut a piece off recently. It's still shiny where the incision was made. Koichi, do you ever use lead in your experiments?'

'No, I have no use for it.'

'Then it must have been the murderer who took some and attached it to the horn of that mask. Though this feels a little light for lead—are you sure that's what it is?'

'Akimitsu, you must be imagining things. A scientist of Professor Chizui's stature would never leave some cheap imitation lying around.'

'Very well. What would an engineer know, eh? When in doubt, always trust the experts! Speaking of which, does anyone else in the household know much chemistry?'

'Rintaro seems to know his way around the darkroom, at least. I'm not too sure about the others ...'

'Ah. $Zn + H_2SO_4 = ZnSO_4 + H_2$ ...'

Muttering this equation to himself, Akimitsu led us out of the laboratory and into the neighbouring study. The walls were lined from floor to ceiling with the Professor's vast collection of scientific literature. As well as a full set of *Chemische Berichte* and *Annalen der Physik*—a rare sight in a private collection like this—there were scholarly works from all over the Western world, together with an astounding array of other journals. If there was a clue to the hidden treasure lurking in this enormous trove of knowledge, finding it would take a superhuman effort.

Framed on the wall over the desk were the following lines, written in English:

All that glisters is not gold;
Often have you heard that told:
Some there be that shadows kiss;
Such have but a shadow's bliss;
You that choose not by the view,
Chance as fair and choose as true!

The text appeared to have been produced by stitching together some of the most famous lines from Shakespeare's *Merchant of Venice*. Creating something from nothing, discovering value in the seemingly worthless—that, of course, was the mission, the calling of the chemist. For example, coal tar, once shunned for its foul smell and polluting nature, was now used as an innovative raw material in modern dyeing processes—with dazzling results. It seemed Professor Chizui had framed Shakespeare's words as a permanent reminder of the dangers of valuing only external beauty—a gesture that, as a fellow chemist, I could not help but admire.

The study did not yield any important clues. I do not think Akimitsu was even necessarily expecting to find any. Rather, it was as though he wanted to soak up the sinister atmosphere that pervaded the Chizui mansion, in the hope of somehow penetrating its secrets.

The three of us made our way up the front stairs, where Akimitsu came to a halt in the hallway. He was standing in front of Taijiro's room, the site of the previous night's murder.

'I think I'd like to take another look at the scene of the crime …'

Little about the room had changed from the previous evening. White powder had been scattered here and there in order to dust for prints, the body had been removed for autopsy, and the mask and key had been seized as evidence. The room felt eerily empty.

'Koichi, what do you think about this locked-room murder, then?'

Akimitsu lit his pipe and gave me a meaningful look.

'Oh, but it's just as you said, Akimitsu—when in doubt, always trust the experts. I thought locked-room murders were your speciality?'

91

'Well, yes—but right now, I'm at a complete loss. See, regardless of how the murder itself is carried out, there are all sorts of ways of sealing a room. But they all require there to be at least some kind of an opening, even if it's only the size of a thread. But this door is completely flush with its frame, and the windows were all closed and locked from inside. The only possibility left are those pivot windows—you said they were open when you left the room last night?'

'Yes. I'm almost certain of that.'

'And I see they don't have locks. Still, when we broke into the room, even they were shut tight. From the inside, opening or closing them is simple—you just pull the cord dangling from the window and it shuts, with a spring closing the latch. Pull it in the other direction and it opens. But what if you wanted to close the window from *outside*?'

'Could it have been pushed shut with a pole or something?'

'Technically possible, I suppose. But the problem then would be where you'd push it from—and how. Reaching the upstairs window of a mansion like this with a pole or rod of some kind would be quite a feat, especially as the pivot windows are located near the ceiling. They must be five or six metres from the ground. Meanwhile, there's nothing that might serve as a handhold on the outer wall; scaling it would be completely impossible. Even if you had a ladder that long, you'd need several people to get it into position. No, there must have been some other way—a method so cunning we can't even imagine it.'

Just then, a thought occurred to me, but something made me hesitate to say it aloud. Presently we left the room and ascended the stairs to the attic. The room directly above Taijiro's was originally used for storage, but had recently been converted into a darkroom. The door was unlocked and swung effortlessly open.

The darkroom had a gently sloping ceiling and a window, reaching almost to the floor, that was fitted with a dark blackout curtain. There was a sink, a red lamp, an enlarger, a guillotine, beakers and trays, together with the other tools and chemicals found in any darkroom. But when Akimitsu peered under the desk on which these items were arranged, he started on the spot.

'Koichi,' he said, glancing up at me, 'looks like we've found those chemicals!'

I leaned over to look, and immediately recognized the two bottles as the zinc and sulphuric acid that had been missing from the laboratory shelf.

But there was something else that drew our attention: the faint smell of jasmine that seemed to hang in the air. Its sweet fragrance seemed remarkably similar to the perfume-like smell that had emanated from Taijiro's body.

As for where it was coming from, we could not be sure. The only explanation that seemed plausible to me was that, having originally been sprayed on some object, it had simply permeated the very air of the darkroom.

Meanwhile, the middle of the wall was plastered with a collection of nude photographs of women, all in such indecent poses that it felt wrong even to look at them. I'd heard Rintaro was a member of a secret club in Yokohama; perhaps he had taken the photos there? One of the women was blonde and French-looking; another, with piercing eyes, had a Jewish appearance. There were Chinese belles, Japanese women with jet-black hair … and, there, in the middle of them all—

'Isn't that … Hisako!' exclaimed Akimitsu.

It was true; there she was. I felt the blood rushing to my head, so violently that I almost lost my balance.

Presumably the photo had been taken after she'd gone mad.

But when had Rintaro persuaded his cousin—his own flesh and blood—to undress and let him photograph her like this?

Normally, no matter how wicked a man becomes, no matter how nihilistic his attitude, some tiny trace of compassion will linger in his heart. But with Rintaro, even that last vestige of humanity seemed to have vanished entirely. I imagined him with some courtesan over a drink, having a good laugh at the photo, and felt a fresh wave of intense hatred for the man. Even Yojiro had averted his eyes. Clearly, when it came to pure callousness and cruelty, his brother was in a different league.

At some point, a heavy shower had begun outside. The rain beat down noisily on the roof above us; occasional flashes of lightning came in through the window, filling the room with a momentary and dizzying purple light. For a while, none of us could speak; we simply stood there in silence. It was almost as though we had forgotten all about the murder the previous evening—or the possibility of a second and a third …

Eventually, we gathered ourselves and made our way out of the darkroom.

'Koichi,' said Akimitsu, tapping me on the shoulder. 'You wouldn't happen to know where the electric and telephone wires enter the house, would you?'

'On the other side of the attic from the darkroom, I believe. The nearest utility pole is on the hill behind that side of the house, you see.'

'I see. So this would be the easiest place from which to access the wiring …'

We descended the stairs, each lost in our thoughts. But as we drew close to Yojiro's room, I noticed something odd hanging from the handle of his door. A piece of string had been fastened to either side of a piece of white card, and on it, in black ink, were the words:

By the time I glanced at him, Yojiro's face was already the colour of ash. Three deep wrinkles had etched themselves into his brow; his hands and feet appeared to be trembling slightly. He took a cigarette from his pocket, but it fell from his hand before he could light it.

'*Second victim …*' Akimitsu read the words in a murmur, but I could see a fiery resolve in his eyes. 'Yojiro, who else is still in the house?'

'Everyone, I think …'

'I see. Well, let's go into your room for now. We can't just ignore a thing like this.'

He wrenched the card from the door handle, then shepherded us into the room, where he began addressing us in a low, barely audible voice:

'Mr Chizui, the murderer has cast down a second gauntlet. Of course, we already knew a second and a third murder were planned, thanks to the order of three coffins. But this is an even more brazen provocation. I refuse to simply twiddle my thumbs. Not only will I stop you from coming to any harm, I'll use this as an opportunity to unmask the murderer.

'Given the ongoing investigation, you can't be seen leaving the house. At the same time, we cannot allow the person responsible for that horrific locked-room murder to act with impunity. So: let the two of us change places tonight. I'll stay in your bedroom and keep a lookout for the murderer while you spend the night at my hotel. Stay away from your room this evening. At ten o'clock, go out to the garden; I will meet you at the gazebo. Koichi here will flip the house's main circuit breaker, and while all the lights are out, I will enter your room in your place.

'Whatever anyone says, Koichi and I are the only ones you can trust. Is that clear? Not even the telephone is safe in this house. We'll return to the hotel for the time being. Stay vigilant this evening, Mr Chizui: your very life may depend on it.'

Akimitsu was speaking so quietly that we had to strain our ears. Yojiro, meanwhile, was increasingly jumpy. As he nodded along to Akimitsu's instructions, thick beads of sweat trickled down his forehead.

'What do you mean, the telephone isn't safe? Could someone be listening in?'

'I believe so. When your father telephoned me yesterday evening, someone managed to eavesdrop on our conversation and record his every word in shorthand. As I say, stay on your guard. The walls in this house have ears. Someone might be listening to us right now.'

'Really?'

'Don't worry. I'll see you this evening.'

Akimitsu rose from his chair, seeming to brim with confidence.

And yet every part of his plan was soon to be dashed to pieces. It wasn't long until the murderer outwitted him, using the same horrific method to claim a second victim.

The rain lifted as abruptly as it had started. To the west, clouds gleamed with the brilliant light of the setting sun, while in the opposite direction a shimmering rainbow arched across a blue patch of sky.

Akimitsu and I returned to the Marine Hotel, where we talked over dinner. But our conversation did not touch on any crucial aspect of the case. It appeared that, unlike the murders he'd encountered in detective novels, Akimitsu was struggling to make head or tail of the events at the Chizui mansion. I must confess that his confusion surprised me. Indeed, I began to feel as though even I might make a better detective.

At around half past seven, I stood up and took my leave. He made no effort to stop me.

'Koichi, tell Yojiro to come to the gazebo at ten o'clock sharp. He mustn't be early or late. I will time my departure so that I get there at five minutes to ten.'

'Yes, I'll see to it. But, Akimitsu, I'm not sure about this circuit breaker idea. If anyone catches me flipping the switch, I'll be in trouble. What if I were to turn on the large electric stove in the laboratory and blow the fuse instead?'

'I'll leave the exact method up to you. Whatever you choose, I'm counting on you, Koichi.'

I nodded and left the hotel. Night had already fallen. Crickets chirped noisily in the bushes lining the road, heralding the arrival of autumn.

It was almost eight o'clock by the time I reached the mansion. Yojiro was in the dining room, making small talk with Sawako and the maids. I told him I had a message from Akimitsu, and led him into the hall where I whispered the instructions into his ear. He nodded gravely, then made his way back into the dining room.

It was later established that, at this time, Rintaro was holed up in his attic darkroom as usual, Sonoe was in bed, while Hisako and Kenkichi were in their room. The front door had been locked from inside, but the rear entrance was open, allowing anyone to walk in or out as they pleased.

Shortly before nine o'clock, I went into the laboratory and made the necessary preparations for later that evening. With that done, I returned to the dining room, where to my surprise, I now found Sawako sitting alone.

'Where's Yojiro?'

'He said he was going to bed and went upstairs. The maids have gone back to their room, too. But Koichi—there's something I wanted to talk to you about.'

So Yojiro hadn't followed Akimitsu's instructions. A cold shiver raced down my spine.

'I'm afraid I'm a little busy at the moment, Sawako. Can we talk later, perhaps?'

'Always running away from me, aren't you?'

She stared up at me reproachfully, but my mind was elsewhere. I rushed out of the dining room and into the garden, where I checked the gazebo. Then I went back into the house and made my way upstairs, where I knocked on Yojiro's door. There was no response. Shuddering with apprehension, I looked in the bathroom, but there was no sign of him there either. Unable to contain myself any longer, I rushed to the telephone booth.

'Akimitsu, something has gone very wrong. I can't find Yojiro.'

'What? Didn't you pass on my instructions?'

'I made them very clear.'

'He was around earlier in the evening, then?'

'He was in the dining room until shortly before nine o'clock, talking to Sawako and the maids. But when I came out of the laboratory at nine, I found Sawako alone in the dining room. She told me he'd gone upstairs to his room. But when I knocked on his door, there was no response.'

'Have you checked the gazebo?'

'Yes.'

'What about the bathroom?'

'No sign of him.'

Akimitsu fell silent for a moment. When he spoke again, the voice that came down the line was grave.

'Koichi, was he wearing a wristwatch?'

'Yes—a Longines, I believe.'

There was another deathly silence. I quite clearly heard Akimitsu gulping for breath.

'Right, it's nine twenty-five now. I'll be there in a shot. Wait for me!'

As I heard him slam the receiver down, I felt suddenly isolated, as though a dark chasm had opened up around me. I went to look in the dining room, but the lights were out and Sawako was nowhere to be seen. With a strange uneasiness in my chest, I opened the door to the maids' room, but found only its two usual inhabitants chattering away.

'Have you seen Sawako?'

'She was in the dining room 'til just now, sir. Have you tried the garden?'

But by now I could barely bring myself to move. Perhaps it was simply cowardice; in any case, a strange terror seemed to have come over me. I sat down and spent the next fifteen minutes or so talking idly with the maids. Then we heard the doorbell ring. Akimitsu was here. Accompanied by one of the maids, I hurried to greet him.

Akimitsu stood in the doorway, his face drained of colour. He was wearing an open-necked shirt and white trousers. In his right hand was a pocket torch; in his left was a cigarette from which he flicked the ashes as he spoke.

'Have you found Yojiro yet?'

'I'm afraid I'm too scared to even look for him any more.'

'Pull yourself together, Koichi. Come on—we'll check the gazebo first.' He turned to the maid. 'Come with us, would you?'

We all hurried out of the rear entrance and into the garden. Swollen banks of cloud hung low over the sea, and the evening

99

air was thick and gloomy, as though another shower might sweep in at any moment. The gazebo stood on a bluff some fifty metres from the house.

Below us curved Tokyo Bay; during the day, the low mountains of southern and central Chiba could be seen quite distinctly on its far side. But this was no time to be admiring the scenery. The beam from Akimitsu's torch swept slowly over the pillars, benches and floor of the gazebo.

'Is that you, Koichi?' came a woman's voice from behind us. 'Are you looking for something?'

It was Sawako. It was just as the maid had suggested: she'd been in the garden the whole time.

'We're looking for Yojiro,' said Akimitsu, spinning around. 'Do you know where he might be?' But when his torch beam found her face, it revealed a strangely doubtful expression.

'I thought he was upstairs?'

'It seems not. Say, Koichi, what's that smell?'

By now, I had noticed it too. The jasmine-like fragrance.

When I had checked the gazebo earlier, I couldn't remember smelling it; and yet now the air around the gazebo was thick with the scent.

Akimitsu's torch continued its slow, stubborn creep across the ground. But we still couldn't see anything out of the ordinary.

We took another step forward. Then, as the light from the torch reached the rocky bluff just beyond the gazebo, Sawako and the maid screamed, their voices ripping through the silent night. Sawako fainted and fell towards me; I scrabbled to catch her, then set her down on a chair in the gazebo.

The torch beam had landed on the pale corpse of Yojiro Chizui. His hands clutched vaguely at the air. The jasmine fragrance seemed to emanate from the body—and across

100

the breast of his white shirt lay a single spray of imitation red maple leaves.

I recalled Mr Ishikari's words as I left the room last night. *What prop did the demon carry onto the stage?*

Next I found myself remembering a line from a Noh play:

Behold! She who was woman has become a fearsome demon …

The play in question was titled *Momijigari*, or 'maple viewing'. And what prop had the demon wielded in that play? A spray of maple leaves …

My turbulent thoughts went unnoticed by Akimitsu, who by contrast seemed remarkably calm. He crouched down to inspect the body, then rose and turned to me.

'No wounds this time either,' he murmured. 'Maybe that's only to be expected, given that he seems to have fallen on the sand between the rocks. It looks like the cause of death was another heart attack. The only part of him that hit the rocks was his left hand—look, his watch has stopped. If it's a Longines, we can assume it kept good time. The hands are stopped at nine twenty-six.'

6

The Buried Crime

(Koichi Yanagi's journal, continued)

The fear and excitement of the first murder had barely had time to settle before a second had been committed. Now, the police could no longer dismiss the deaths as natural, or attempt to ascribe them to some ghostly phenomenon. The telephone call to the undertaker had been no prank. They were left with no choice but to ramp up their investigation.

My own position seemed quite shaky. Apart from the maids, I was the only potential suspect who wasn't a family member—and in both murders, I'd been one of the last people to see the victim alive. Luckily, at nine twenty-six, the assumed time of Yojiro's death, I'd only just got off the phone with Akimitsu—and of course I had an alibi for the first murder, too. I shuddered to think of the peril I'd be in if Sawako hadn't vouched for me that evening; it was no exaggeration to say that she had saved me. She would have known full well that suspicion might fall on her, and how dangerous that could make things for her—and still she had spoken out on my behalf. I was overcome with gratitude. Solving the mystery of the Chizui family as soon as possible would, I reasoned, be the best way of repaying her good deed.

Still, why had Yojiro ignored Akimitsu's advice and gone out to the gazebo almost an hour earlier than he was supposed to? His watch was Swiss-made; it seemed reasonable to assume it kept good time. The only other person in the garden had been Sawako—and what's more, we knew she'd been near the gazebo at nine twenty-six. It was hard to deny the evidence against her. Indeed, the police seemed to have her pegged as the prime suspect. But I had my own role to play. I was convinced I must help her out of danger. And so, the day after the second murder, with Akimitsu at my side, I paid a visit to Mr Ishikari.

When we walked into his room, tucked away at the back of the Yokohoma District Prosecutors' Office, he greeted us with a doleful expression. The investigation into the Chizui murders appeared to be taking its toll on his mental well-being.

'Thank you for coming,' he said, half-rising from his desk. 'Mr Takagi, Koichi has told me about you. I'll be most grateful if you gentlemen are able to shed any light on these killings.'

We each relayed everything we had learned so far. But Mr Ishikari's expression remained downcast. I decided it was time to share what was on my mind.

'Mr Ishikari, there *is* one thing that's been troubling me. You see, Professor Chizui's death ten years ago was also due to a heart attack, wasn't it?'

Akimitsu stared at me in surprise. Mr Ishikari opened up a notebook on his desk.

'That's right. He died on the sixth of September ten years ago, at the same mansion. The cause of death was indeed a heart attack.'

'But he'd injured himself before that, hadn't he?'

'I see you're well acquainted with the case. Yes, it seems a glass flask exploded during one of his experiments.'

'Mr Ishikari, the glassware used by chemists is designed never to break, no matter how high you set the burner. But, as a scientist, I also happen to know that glass flasks are sometimes cleaned with ether. Now, given its flammability, ether is normally kept well clear of any scientific experiment, but if even a minuscule amount of it were to linger inside the flask after it had been cleaned, and it was then heated with the burner—well, an explosion would be inevitable ...'

'Koichi, what are you saying? Surely you don't mean ...'

'Don't get me wrong—this is merely a hypothetical scenario. I was away travelling at the time of the Professor's death, and it was only two years later that I learned about this particular hazard of ether. Still, for a scientist of Professor Chizui's stature to commit such a basic error seemed unthinkable to me—and yet in the end, the police chalked the accident up to just such an oversight. Now, do you have a record of who was staying at the mansion at the time of the accident?'

Mr Ishikari consulted the notebook. 'It seems the Professor was there with his entire immediate family. Taijiro, Rintaro and Yojiro were also visiting.'

'And while the Professor was recovering from the injuries he received to his face and upper body, he died of a heart attack. Meanwhile, of the three guests who were visiting the mansion back then, two have now died of heart attacks of their own. Don't you feel there might be some sinister explanation behind all this?'

'Koichi ...' By now Mr Ishikari's eyes were burning with interest.

'Mr Ishikari, who drew up the Professor's death certificate?'

'It says here it was a doctor who happened to be visiting Taijiro at the time—in fact, he was staying at the Marine Hotel. His name is Saburo Oka.'

'Indeed. Now, Doctor Oka runs a private mental asylum in Ogikubo, in western Tokyo. For the past ten years, the Professor's wife, Kayoko Chizui, has been one of his patients. Not only that, but two nights ago, immediately after the call to the Marine Hotel, someone made a long-distance call to the Oka Asylum.'

Mr Ishikari stared wordlessly at me.

'Yesterday, Yojiro told us that the Professor hid the family fortune, valued at tens of millions of yen, probably somewhere in the Chizui mansion; its location remains unknown. Yojiro was under the mistaken impression that he and his siblings have a claim to the treasure, but that remains a fantasy on his part. No matter how frail their bodies or minds, as long as the Professor's wife and children are alive, they are his rightful heirs. Now, with the Professor long dead, who else could possibly know where he hid the family fortune?'

'His wife, I suppose. But, as you know, she went insane a long time ago …'

'Actually, she's in a mental asylum—which isn't quite the same thing. In fact, that's just the problem. I believe this to be the hidden piece of the puzzle—the secret behind the Chizui family's tragedy. Please, indulge my imagination a little further. Hisako, as we know, is genuinely deranged. So—why hasn't the family put *her* in a mental asylum?'

'Koichi, you can't possibly …'

Mr Ishikari looked at me fearfully, his face a ghostly pale.

'That's right. Quite the paradox, isn't it? Though really, it's hard to fault the logic. After all, if you aren't going to send a genuine lunatic to a mental asylum, then who *would* you send? Well, someone of perfectly sound mind.

'Gentlemen, Japan is changing: we have a democracy now; the military has been disbanded; the police are no longer the violent enforcers we knew in the past. It seems that even in prisons, with a few rare exceptions, torture has fallen out of use. These days, there is only one place where such brutality is still permitted—the mental asylum.

'This is possible, of course, because we hold doctors in higher regard than almost any other profession. We see them as somehow special—almost holy, if you like. But any privilege, in the wrong hands, can have terrible consequences. And when a doctor abuses their power, the results can be spine-chilling.

'I am talking about a truly heinous crime, one that makes ordinary murder seem like child's play. It is a violation of humanity itself; a revolt against the divine order; a defilement of everything we hold sacred.

'You see, a patient at a mental asylum is cut off entirely from the outside world. Even prison inmates are allowed to meet their family, but once someone is diagnosed with severe mental illness, they lose contact with everyone but the doctor and a few nurses. Now, say that doctor, blinded by greed, were to betray his sacred profession and stray from the path of righteousness for the sake of a few million yen—well, then the very maw of hell would open up, and the scene would be set for a tragedy of nightmarish proportions. Gentlemen, the crime I am referring to may be buried in the past, but that doesn't mean we should let it remain that way. I am begging you: for the sake of justice, help me uncover the truth.'

As soon as I had finished talking, Mr Ishikari got to his feet. He was visibly agitated. As he stood by the window, gazing at the dense shrubbery outside, I even thought I saw tears glistening in his eyes.

'That's a highly speculative theory, Koichi. Still, I can't help feeling there might be some truth to it. From the bottom of my heart, I hope you're wrong. But no matter how awful the reality, or how much suspicion we arouse, we must get to the bottom of this … Wait here, you two. I'll get in touch with Tokyo.'

With this, Mr Ishikari left the office. We awaited his return with bated breath. Thirty long minutes went by, and then an hour. Finally, he reappeared.

'Right, I made some calls. We need to get to that asylum on the double. I've asked the local police to secure Mrs Chizui's ward. Come on, you two, there's no time to lose!'

Without another word, we rushed out of the building and into the car we'd kept waiting. The driver revved the engine into life. We sped off through the sun-bleached streets of Yokohama; houses, telephone poles, people and bicycles flitted past our window, appearing and disappearing in an instant. Before long we had left the city behind. But our minds were too preoccupied even to talk, let alone enjoy the scenery. Mr Ishikari leaned forward in his seat, his bloodshot eyes riveted on the road ahead of us. Even Akimitsu seemed too anxious to light his pipe.

'Driver, can't you go any faster? There's no time to waste!'

The car accelerated. The trees lining the road began to blur past like so much chaff in the wind. And yet even this exhilarating speed felt, to our impatient trio, like the slow crawl of an ant.

Just a little further, I kept telling myself, though I barely even registered the route we were taking. By the time we lurched around the final curve and screeched to a halt in front of the Oka Asylum, I was breathless with anxiety.

A policeman and a detective came rushing over to greet Mr Ishikari as he leapt from the car.

'Well? How is she?'

'We might have been too late, sir,' replied the detective. 'She's fading fast—though that's hardly surprising, given how they've been treating her here.'

'But is she sane or insane?'

'Well, she's in a terrible state right now. Our doctor has been administering a heart stimulant, but he doesn't think she'll last much longer. She looked very relieved to see us—perhaps now she feels she can finally let go. But yes, she still seemed quite sane to me …'

We'd heard all we needed to hear. Brushing the voluble detective to one side, we rushed into the asylum. Inside, shrill laughter echoed from the wards. A female patient flung herself at me in an attempted embrace; a young man, completely naked, stood on his hands and cackled at us. But these sights did not distract our attention. Guided by the detective, we made our way down several long halls, ducking through a series of iron grill doors, until we reached one of the innermost wards.

Could it even be called a ward? There was a small barred window high up on the wall, through which even the summer sunshine seemed reluctant to enter. The tatami mats were mouldy, an acrid stench of unknown origin assaulted our nostrils, and leaking water had smeared the walls a miserable grey. Even prison inmates were surely treated more humanely than this. I recalled my army days, and the dreaded guardhouse to which disobedient soldiers were confined—and yet even that paled in comparison to the wretched sight in front of us.

In one corner, fast asleep under a grubby, fraying blanket, was an emaciated old woman. With her sunken eyes, hollow cheeks and white head of hair, she resembled nothing more than a living corpse. And yet even in this moribund state, I immediately discerned the figure of Kayoko Chizui.

'This is Doctor Morimoto. He's with us,' said the detective, indicating the middle-aged man in a white gown who was squatting at Kayoko's side to take her pulse.

'Can't she be taken to a cleaner ward?' Mr Ishikari demanded fiercely. The doctor simply shook his head in response—and yet his eyes seemed to convey some deeper meaning, one he could not express in words. As if picking up on this silent communication, Mr Ishikari took a step forward.

'Doctor, is she … sane?'

'In this state, it's hard to tell. In any case, it's a miracle she's still alive. She seemed glad to see us—like she realized she'd finally been saved. But she's been fast asleep since then. I doubt she'll last another two hours. If we'd only found her a month, even a week earlier …'

Just then, Kayoko slowly opened her eyes. They seemed to be searching for some final light.

'You … you … !' she cried with fierce desperation, as if summoning her last reserves of energy. But then her voice grew quieter.

'Eighty-eight in eighty-two … Eighty-eight in eighty-two …'

By now she was whispering.

'Portia …'

These were the last words she managed to utter clearly. But, having leaned in closer than anyone else, I thought I caught a faint, final utterance, one which nobody else appeared to hear …

Doctor Morimoto checked her pulse again, then looked up at us with a grave expression and shook his head.

'May she rest in peace.'

Tears were trickling down my face. I wasn't alone in my grief: Akimitsu was crying too, and even Mr Ishikari seemed to have set aside his role as prosecutor and was simply weeping as a fellow human. I knew what he must be going through; faced with a scene like this, could anyone have held back their tears? I felt my respect for him growing even deeper. For all his reputation as a ruthless prosecutor of the law, I could see that, at his core, Mr Ishikari was a deeply compassionate man.

We prayed in front of the body, then wrenched ourselves away from the room. We'd been too late. If only we'd acted a little more swiftly, we might have been able to establish definitively whether Kayoko had been sane all along; now she was gone for ever.

Was my theory doomed to remain just that—a theory? Even allowing for recent scientific advances, evaluating an individual's mental health based on an autopsy alone is an extremely difficult task. Of course, Doctor Oka and his staff would be questioned. But with Kayoko dead, they would be sure to deny any accusations outright, and we'd struggle to ever bring them to justice. In the face of this horrific crime, the law seemed absolutely powerless.

Still, I had one last hope. Those words Kayoko had uttered with her final breaths: *Eighty-eight in eighty-two … Portia …*

Could they really just have been the ravings of a lunatic? If I could only prove that these words contained some hidden meaning, that would provide a degree of psychological backing for my theory that she was sane. But what on earth could that meaning be? I decided I would stop at nothing to answer this question.

'Don't worry, sir,' said the detective, in an attempt to console the dejected Mr Ishikari. 'We'll take Doctor Oka and the nurses into custody and get them to confess everything.'

But Mr Ishikari simply hung his head in silence. Eventually, he murmured: 'Back to my office.'

Once again, our car raced through the sunshine-flooded streets. This time, however, our hearts were like lead.

'That was some real insight you showed today, Koichi,' said Mr Ishikari. 'But we missed our chance—and by a hair's breadth. I wonder if there isn't some other way of penetrating the family's mysterious past?'

'Well, there is one other lead I can think of ... Mr Ishikari, it seems all but certain that Kayoko was sane. But if Hisako *didn't* have a madwoman for a mother, then what triggered her own insanity? Everyone has always assumed it was hereditary, but if that isn't the case, I fear the answer might reveal some other terrible secret. At this point, don't you think a thorough medical report on the entire family might be useful?'

Some of the colour had returned to Mr Ishikari's face. 'You know, Koichi, I think you might be right. Fortunately, the family physician, Doctor Yamamoto, happens to be an old school friend of mine. Even if officially it's a no-go, I'm sure he'll help me in a private capacity. Why didn't I think of this earlier? Driver, stop by that police box, would you?'

The car lurched to a halt and he leapt out. Before he dashed inside, I called out: 'Mr Ishikari, I'd like to try a little experiment with that Noh mask. Do you think you could ask the police to return it to the mansion tomorrow?'

Fifteen minutes later, Mr Ishikari got back into the car. 'I spoke to Doctor Yamamoto on the phone. He's on his way to my office. Let's hurry!'

My mind was preoccupied by other thoughts. Those two phrases—'eighty-eight in eighty-two' and 'Portia'—were swirling around in my head, competing for my attention, as though they were desperately trying to tell me something. I was convinced I was a step away from solving everything—and yet that breakthrough remained tantalizingly out of reach.

When we got back to Mr Ishikari's office, we found Doctor Yamamoto already waiting for us. I had briefly encountered him on the night of the first murder, but we hadn't been formally introduced. Once the greetings were out of the way, Mr Ishikari began to speak in a low voice.

'Doctor, I asked you to come here today because I'd like your personal opinion on something. I won't be recording our conversation, and Koichi and Mr Takagi are simply here to help me out with the investigation. So please, relax. Imagine it's just the two of us having a chat.'

'Hiroyuki, doctors are sworn to the strictest secrecy when it comes to anything they learn about their patients in a professional capacity. Even in a court of law, I have an obligation—and the right—not to betray that confidentiality. But this does seem like a rather unique situation. Firstly, there's the fact that it's you, my old friend, asking so earnestly for my help. Second, with these ghastly murders at the Chizui household, I feel I have a duty towards society to reveal everything I know—indeed, it seems the only decent thing to do. So, tell me what you need to know, and I'll fill you in as best as I can.'

All of a sudden, the doctor's expression had lost its usual mildness. Instead, his tightly pursed lips indicated a fierce resolve.

'Thank you, Doctor. First of all, was Yojiro Chizui's death also due to a heart attack?'

'Yes. As with the first murder, no other cause seems possible.'

'Still, it seems very unlikely that two members of a family would die from heart attacks on consecutive evenings, doesn't it? From a medical perspective, is there any way a heart attack could be artificially triggered?'

'Several such methods have been reported in the past. But if the victims were drugged, the substance would remain in their bodies after death. If the autopsies indicate no such traces, we can rule that out.'

112

'In both murders, there was a strong smell of jasmine emanating from the body. Do you think the perfume could have contained some unknown poison?'

'Medically speaking, that doesn't seem possible. No, I don't think this was some new method. It must be something obvious—something we doctors know all about, but which I'm failing to see. I imagine that when we find out what it was, we'll be astounded by how simple it was—even as we shudder with horror.'

'What about a psychological shock?'

'Tell me, Hiroyuki: do you think fear is something we can measure on a scale? Imagine encountering a snake: one person might faint, while another looks on coolly. This idea of a death-inducing fright, of a shock so great it stops the victim's very heart from beating—it might sound plausible, but believe me, it'd be almost impossible to pull off.'

'Well, do let me know if you think of anything. Now, about Hisako—do you know where her madness might have come from?'

'This part is a little hard for me to tell you. You see, it appears she was carrying a latent disease, which was then activated by an intense shock of some kind.'

This was something I had vaguely suspected. But to hear it from the mouth of an expert like this was truly harrowing. Mr Ishikari, too, furrowed his brow and began fiddling restlessly with his pencil. Akimitsu, silent until now, took over the questioning.

'This ... disease—was *that* something she inherited?'

'I don't believe so. When Hisako was born, I took blood samples from the Professor and his wife and found nothing out of the ordinary. She must have acquired it at some later point. Normally, when the disease in question is latent, it takes at least a decade for the pathology to develop to the point of insanity. But if the patient experiences an abnormally intense shock, it is not unknown for madness to set in within a few years. Unfortunately, I believe that may have been the case with Hisako.'

This, too, I had dimly surmised. But hearing it out loud, it felt as though I were sinking into some cold abyss.

'Gentlemen,' continued the doctor, 'Hisako is not a virgin. I have no way of knowing who is responsible, but it seems that around eight or nine years ago, she surrendered herself to someone heavily infected with the disease.'

These words were like the final nail in the coffin. We couldn't even bring ourselves to speak. It felt as though we'd been clubbed in the back of the head.

'Doctor,' murmured Mr Ishikari despondently, 'do you have the family's medical history to hand?'

'I drew up some notes after the first murder took place, in case they might be useful—here.'

The doctor produced a sheet of paper from his bag and unfolded it on the table. We began poring over its every word.

Sonoe Chizui (76): Stepmother of Soichiro and mother of Taijiro Chizui. High blood pressure; mild stroke; close monitoring required. Left side of body moderately impaired. Blood type: O. Syphilis test: negative.

Taijiro Chizui (54): Sonoe's son. No heart abnormalities. Blood type: O. Syphilis test: negative.

Rintaro Chizui (32): Taijiro's older son. Almost no sense of smell due to severe empyema. Blood type: O. Syphilis test: highly positive.

Yojiro Chizui (30): Taijiro's second son. No heart abnormalities. Blood type: A. Syphilis test: negative.

Sawako Chizui (28): Taijiro's daughter. No heart abnor-
malities. Blood type: AB. Syphilis test: negative.
Hisako Chizui (27): Soichiro's daughter. Disease-induced
mental impairment, treatment likely impossible.
Blood type: A. Syphilis test: highly positive.
Kenkichi Chizui (14): Soichiro's son. Valvular heart
disease, treatment likely impossible. Blood type: A.
Syphilis test: negative.

The doctor's notes revealed several sinister facts. With their
cold medical precision, these brief words shook me more than
a thousand others ever could.

'But,' gasped Akimitsu, 'this suggests that the only other
person in the Chizui family with syphilis is Rintaro. And I found
a nude photograph of Hisako in his darkroom. In which case ...'

'Mr Takagi, that is conjecture. As a doctor, I cannot in good
faith either confirm or deny what you are suggesting.'

'When I first met Rintaro at the mansion, he began bom-
barding me with a series of absurd theories. I suppose he must
be on the brink of insanity himself?'

'Indeed, that is one of the disease's symptoms. As has often
been said, there is a fine line between genius and insanity. As
the disease progresses, the patient begins to undergo persistent delusions. Now, when those strange visions inhabit the
mind of someone who was a genius to begin with, the result
can be a dazzling, if brief, flowering of creativity. Nietzsche's
writings on Zarathustra and the *Übermensch*; Maupassant's
enigmatic yet trenchant masterpieces of the short-story form;
Woodrow Wilson's dream of a world united by the League of
Nations: these beautiful, transcendent ideas were, in a sense,
the product of their crumbling genius being stimulated by
millions of bacteria.

'But of course, such a phenomenon is limited to a mere handful of individuals—those of an extraordinary mental calibre. When someone whose intellect is only marginally higher than average falls victim to the disease, the seeds of tragedy are sown.

'Rintaro's inflated sense of self; his perception of himself as a genius or "*Übermensch*"; his scorn for others; his defiance of the law, social order and morality; his self-deification; his assumption that everyone else should prostrate themselves at his powerful feet—all these can only be explained as the effects of the disease.

'Yes, he is a lunatic of sorts. In that sense, he is probably the most dangerous member of the Chizui family. Hisako, on the other hand, simply has no awareness of her own mental condition—and has been treated as a lunatic from the outset. She poses no great danger to society.

'If a sane person is mistakenly put in a mental asylum, they will endlessly protest their sanity, and assume everyone else around them to be insane. Now, that is indeed a tragedy—but it remains an individual one. But Rintaro is the opposite, in that he mistakenly believes himself to be sane. And as long as those around him believe likewise, the tragedy that awaits is of much graver consequence. It becomes the tragedy of a family, of a society—indeed, of a country.

'Japan owes its current dire predicament, at least in part, to the collective derangement that possessed its former leaders. Just look at the war crimes tribunal now taking place in Tokyo: that deranged spiritualist Shumei Okawa helped sway the nation's spiritual compass for over a decade. Or think of Shakespeare's Hamlet: if we believe him to be sane, the tragedy is merely personal, but if we believe him to be insane, the play becomes the even more appalling tragedy of an entire family.

'My apologies, gentlemen. I get worked up like this some-times. I'm sure you knew all that anyway—please, ignore my ramblings.'

The doctor seemed to be attempting to make light of the situation, and yet there was no doubting the truth lurking in his words. What else lay at the root of the Chizui family's tragedy, if not Rintaro's delusions? Eleven years ago, he had spent a summer in Manchuria; ever since, his behaviour had defied all accepted norms.

'Let's return to these notes of yours,' said Mr Ishikari. 'It appears Sonoe is not Soichiro's real mother?'

'That's right. The Professor's mother died when he was three. Sonoe married into the Chizui family afterwards. She's quite the stubborn old lady. I suppose that's only natural in one's old age, but from what I hear, she's always been rather strong-willed. Apparently she caused Soichiro all sorts of problems in relation to his marriage. Not that his fiancée was from a particularly unsuitable family—but Sonoe still made a big fuss over the importance of the family name and kept insisting that he find someone of equal stock ...'

'I see. And what about Hisako's sudden descent into mad-ness? Do you know what kind of shock might have triggered it?'

'Yes, I have an idea—though I should say this is only con-jecture, and only Hisako herself will know the real reason. Six years ago, she was engaged to the second son of Viscount Kasumi. I'm sure you've all heard of the viscount: he used to be a major string-puller in both the political and business worlds. He's barred from public office now, but he was almost made a cabinet minister during the war. Of course, Taijiro's idea was to gain political influence by marrying off Hisako to him. He was like that, you see—incapable of considering a situation with anything other than personal gain in mind.

'Now, I don't know whether there was ever a formal marriage proposal—perhaps they never got any further than preliminary talks. Either way, not long afterwards, the son died in a fighter plane in the South Pacific. I heard Hisako went mad as soon as word of his death reached her.'

'It says here that Rintaro has severe empyema,' continued Mr Ishikari. 'Would he be able to smell that jasmine fragrance?'

'I don't think so. He's not even able to detect a strong ammonia solution.'

'And there's no chance he might be feigning the condition?'

'Impossible. It's quite easy to test a patient's olfactory abilities. Does this have something to do with the case?'

'It might, and it might not. Now, I have one more question—about the blood types. You see, something's been bothering me. Blood types can't prove parenthood, but they *can* be used to rule it out—even I know that much. So tell me about Taijiro's children. It says here he's a type O, as is Rintaro, while Yojiro is a type A. You haven't recorded their mother's blood type here, as she's deceased, but if the father is O and his two sons are O and A respectively, we can assume she was a type A. Sawako, on the other hand, is the only one in the family with type AB. And yet it's common knowledge that, whatever the partner's blood type, it's impossible for an O-type parent to have AB-type children.'

Doctor Yamamoto abruptly rose from his chair.

'You're right, Hiroyuki. Sawako isn't Taijiro's daughter. She might share a mother with her siblings, but she doesn't have a drop of Chizui blood in her veins.'

118

7

Third Act

We had learned a great deal in the course of the day. Of course, we were yet to fully penetrate the secrets of the Chizui family's past; still, we now knew that the murders that had occurred within the family could only be understood against the backdrop of the various hidden crimes we had uncovered.

I'd managed to gain an insight into the Professor's mysterious death, reveal the truth behind his wife's supposed insanity, explain the causes of Hisako's own madness and confirm that Sawako was not, in fact, Taijiro's daughter. These were all suspicions I had harboured for a long time, but to have bolstered them with facts, and thereby to have impressed them onto Mr Ishikari and Akimitsu, felt like an achievement that would be crucial to solving the case—or at least so I hoped. Then there were those words uttered by Kayoko, which even I had not been expecting.

Eighty-eight in eighty-two and *Portia*.

If my theory was correct and Kayoko had been sane all this time, then these words were surely a vital clue. It was a mystery I felt compelled to solve. And yet I couldn't help feeling that I might have overstepped the mark today—after all, I was supposed to be playing a supporting role, and yet I had begun to act like the protagonist. But Akimitsu didn't seem the least bit bothered.

'My dear Koichi,' he said, patting me on the shoulder as we were about to part ways outside the Marine Hotel, 'I must say I'm rather impressed by your deductive talents. All this time, I've been prattling on about being the Japanese Philo Vance, but just look at what you achieved today. Why not give up the chemistry and become a private detective? I'll be your chronicler if you like—your Watson, your Van Dine. How about a drink to celebrate?'

My mind was still occupied by the mystery of the family, but I wasn't going to spurn his praise. I followed him up to his hotel room, where he cracked open a bottle of his favourite whisky and offered me a glass.

'Koichi, a toast to your talents and future. Go on, drink it down. I'm afraid I don't have much by way of snacks, but how about these canned sardines? ... Anyway, that Chizui family really are a despicable lot, aren't they! The Professor's wife *was* sane, I'm sure of it—and yet they locked her up in a mental asylum for a whole decade ... You know, these murders are probably no less than they deserve. I suppose the killer must be Rintaro or Sawako, but I'm not even sure I feel like stopping them any more. Much easier to wait for the final murder, then arrest whoever's left over, don't you think? How about another drink? This whisky isn't too bad, is it ...'

By now he was on his fourth or fifth glass and seemed quite drunk, not to mention high on his own jabber. His eyes had glazed over slightly, while his cheeks had taken on an almost rouge-like flush.

'I've had plenty already. Akimitsu, thank you for bearing with me today—I know I took over slightly. Tell me though, is your money on Rintaro or Sawako?'

'Sawako, if you really want to know. Firstly, there's the fact that she knows shorthand. Secondly, consider her movements on the night of the first murder: she walked past the telephone booth, went upstairs and into the room where the Noh mask is kept, then down the rear staircase and out into the garden: it's exactly the route I'd expect the murderer to have taken. As for the second murder, she was with Yojiro in the dining room, so she could easily have lured him out to the gazebo. And we know she was in the garden at nine twenty-six—the time of his death.

'Her motive seems plausible, too. She's just like the culprit in *The Greene Murder Case*, you see. Years of psychological pressure, coupled with a desire for material gain—not to mention the fact that she's not even Taijiro's child. In fact, I'm surprised she hasn't pretended to have survived an attempt on her own life, like Van Dine's murderer. I'm sure Rintaro will be the next to go—and with that monster gone from the world, we'll all be able to breathe a little easier. The country's getting overpopulated anyway. Go on, Koichi, have another.'

But now that I'd got him to confess his suspicions, I was done listening to his rambling. I rose and made to leave.

'You're off already?' he asked, looking up at me reprovingly.

'Yes, I think I'll call it a night. Oh, about that note written in shorthand—you still haven't shown it to anyone, have you?'

'Oh, that? Of course not—it's the ace up my sleeve, I only get one chance to play it. Come on—one more glass!'

I couldn't bear to listen to his nonsense a minute longer. Once I had finally managed to extricate myself from his room, I practically fled from the hotel.

Within fifteen minutes or so, the effects of the whisky had just about worn off. When I arrived back at the house, my legs still a little wobbly, one of the maids immediately called out to me.

'Sir, Rintaro was looking for you. He'd like to see you in his room.'

The moment I'd been waiting for was here. I might not have expected him to make the first move, but at this point I still felt prepared. Whatever came to pass, our coexistence in this world was beginning to feel like a preordained impossibility.

I knocked quietly on his door.

'Come in.'

I found him sitting in an armchair puffing on a pipe. His snake-like glare seemed to coil itself immediately around my entire body.

'Tell me, Koichi, where were you today?' he asked, his voice brimming with unconcealed hostility.

'I went to see Mr Ishikari at his office.'

'And then you paid a visit to the Oka Asylum, didn't you? Tell me—was my aunt still alive?'

So he knew how we had spent the day. I felt a momentary shudder, as though it were not a human staring at me but some kind of reptile.

'As fate would have it, she was already at death's door when we arrived.'

'I see. Well, that's a pity.'

His lips had curled into a cold, barely perceptible sneer, one that seemed to mock all of our efforts that day.

'Yes, it really was. If we'd only been a little earlier, we'd have proof that she was quite sane. I imagine that would have been rather inconvenient for some people.'

'It's no concern of mine whether my aunt was sane or insane, Koichi. My father was the one who arranged for her to be hospitalized. In any case, the thing about most humans is this: if they're not insane, they're usually stupid. If they don't end up in a mental asylum, they might as well walk around town ringing a bell for children to laugh at.'

'Be that as it may, on the night of the first murder, I stood outside your father's room and overheard you and your father discussing whether to kill someone. You wouldn't object if I told the police about that, then?'

Rintaro didn't bat an eyelid. 'Eavesdropping, eh? How very like you. I don't remember any discussion of the sort! Listening in on private conversations, inviting prosecutors and detectives into our home—what's compelling you to do all this, Koichi? Why can't you just stay put in that laboratory of yours and make sweeteners like we asked you to?'

'What, and let justice go unserved? No—as a member of society, I have a duty to prevent murders, and to unmask anyone responsible for them.'

'Ah. You and your *justice* again.' His cold sneer still in place, Rintaro blew a series of smoke rings into the air. 'I have to say, I take a rather different view of these murders. In fact, I've found them remarkably stimulating.

'Tell me, Koichi, have you read *The Suicide Club*, by Robert Louis Stevenson? A bunch of complete down-and-outs with nothing left to live for get together and draw cards to determine who is to be killed—and who will do the killing. Their one remaining thrill in life is the pulse-raising horror of the game—the chill that runs down their spine as the cards are revealed one by one.

'But it's not only the dregs of society who get to experience that kind of exhilaration. Perhaps you're familiar with the story of Damocles? Once there was a man who envied the king's sumptuous lifestyle so much that he declared he'd give anything just to live like him for one day. The king hears of his wish and, for some reason, allows him to do so. The man is over the moon. A lavish banquet is held in his honour, but at the height of his merriment, he notices a large sword suspended over his head by a thin rope. All his drunken pleasure immediately vanishes; he turns pale and jumps down from the throne. The king laughs and says: "So, do you understand what it's like to be me?" Now, the story is normally interpreted as a warning about the constant peril that accompanies any position of power—but I've always seen it slightly differently. I think the king had become numb to ordinary sources of stimulation—and his one remaining thrill came from knowing that the sword could fall on his own head at any moment.

'Koichi, now I know how that king felt. Drinking, women, gambling—these days, such things fail to excite me. But the notion that I might be murdered at any time—now *that* is something that can still arouse my interest! Don't worry, though—I won't give in without a fight. You see, I have a decent idea who's behind these murders—and how they pulled them off. I'm confident victory will be mine. I already have a secret weapon of sorts at my disposal—and by that I don't mean I'm planning to kill the murderer in self-defence. No, I'd rather leave that part to somebody else.'

'Oh, I'm sure you have a *very* good idea of how the murders were pulled off. After all, you were staying at this mansion ten years ago when the Professor passed away—and he died of a mysterious heart attack too, didn't he?'

'Koichi, why do you keep implying my uncle's death was murder? Anyway, he was cremated and buried ten years ago; it's not like you can bring him back. Do you even have any proof for your claim? And how could you ever hope to prosecute such an old crime?'

'I think you'll find the statute of limitations for murder cases is fifteen years. Not that it matters. Our human law may insist

124

on such technicalities, but the judgement of heaven knows no such bounds. Once an individual is addicted to power, he can't help but repeat his past crimes—and by the time he realizes fate has abandoned him, it's already too late. We dig our own graves, Rintaro. Ten years after the Professor's death, two more unexplained deaths have occurred in the Chizui mansion. Word will soon get out. And it won't be long until the culprit is arrested.'

'Oh, but that's precisely what I'd like to happen! You know, I'd be careful if I were you, Koichi. I don't think I've ever seen someone so convinced of their own infallibility. Don't worry, though—I'll have you shuddering in fear before too long. And by then it'll be too late to get down at my feet and beg for mercy.'

'We'll see who ends up begging for mercy. At any rate, my work at this house is almost done—and I certainly don't plan on sticking around to make sweeteners. In two days, I'll take my leave of this place. In the meantime, I intend to finish what I've started and bring the curtain down on the tragedy of the Chizui family.'

'My, what confidence. Very well—let me offer a grand finale to rival yours. In two days' time, I will reveal the identity of the murderer. One o'clock in the afternoon, in the dining room.'

'I was going to propose something similar myself. So be it: one o'clock, the day after tomorrow. I'll make my own declaration then too.'

Rintaro fixed me with his gaze; there was an otherworldly, almost phosphorescent gleam in his eyes. And yet I felt confident that this time I would prevail. I knew what he was plotting. Ours was a duel to the death.

'Do you really think anyone else will take you in?' he muttered spitefully, after a pause.

'That is none of your concern.'

'I suppose you're right. If anything, it'll be the court that decides what to do with you.'

There was nothing left to say. I stood up, bowed and left the room.

In the hall I found Sawako waiting, her face pale. Her white blouse and light blue skirt exuded a youthful charm that seemed incongruous in someone so recently and doubly bereaved.

'Koichi, Grandmother is in a terrible state. She's been moaning in her sleep, raving about this and that, and her temperature's almost thirty-nine degrees ... Could you come and have a look?'

I did as she asked. Even from the hallway I could hear a faint, low groaning coming from Sonoe's room. The muffled voice seemed almost to swell up from underground, like the last murmurs of some moribund beast. I took a breath, then opened the door.

The old woman lay half asleep in her bed. Gone was the fiery energy we'd seen the night before last; her wrinkled face was pallid and beaded with sweat, while fear and shock had etched themselves into her features. In her rasping breath I heard the portent of swiftly approaching death. All of a sudden, she clutched a writhing hand to her chest and began to cry out:

'I see it! The mask, the mask! Soichiro, Kayoko, it wasn't me! I didn't know! It was Rintaro—Rintaro planned it all! I didn't do it! What? That wasn't me either ... Hisako, is that you? Trying to scare me with that mask, are you? How dare you harass an old lady like me ... What's that flowery smell ... I can feel the wind ...'

Sawako had turned deathly pale. I couldn't help but shudder. One by one, the various layers of the Chizui family's tragic past were being peeled away. Sonoe's spirited obstinacy, her insistence on never appearing weak—it had all been an empty performance. In her nightmares she was unable to escape the judgement of heaven and hell. She had to have known the truth behind the Professor's death—and now, with two more murders taking place under similar circumstances a decade later, she seemed gripped by fear and remorse.

Kenkichi had entered the room at some point, and now stood in the corner, staring at us. I put a hand to the old woman's forehead. It was scorching hot.

'Grandmother, wake up!' said Sawako, shaking her frantically. 'It's me, Sawako.'

Eventually Sonoe's sunken eyelids opened.

'Was I asleep? I had an awful nightmare … Hisako was wearing the Noh mask. Said I had killed her father. I told her it wasn't true, but she wouldn't listen. She kept following me about … You!' She seemed to have finally noticed my presence. 'What are *you* doing here? I heard all about your little trip to the Oka Asylum, you know.'

'I see. And who might have told you, I wonder?'

'Rintaro. Listen, boy, if you want to keep living in our house, I'd keep your nose out of our affairs.'

'Grandmother!' said Sawako, gripping her arm.

'Perhaps I was a little indiscreet today,' I said. 'Still, that indiscretion supplied me with near-certain evidence that Kayoko was sane all along. Though I suppose you didn't know anything about that, did you?'

Sonoe jerked up from her bed like she'd received an electric shock. In the middle of her puckered and otherwise lifeless face, her two eyes blazed like hot coals.

'Get out of our house! No one who talks that way is welcome in this family. I never want to see you again.'

'Oh, don't worry—I was planning on leaving anyway. Still, I have an appointment to keep with Rintaro. At one o'clock on the day after tomorrow, I will reveal the identity of the murderer. And after that, madam, I will leave this place for good.'

Sawako, more than Sonoe, appeared shocked by these words. She shot me a burning look.

'You're leaving us, Koichi? And even more importantly, do you really know who the murderer is?'

'I'm fairly certain, yes. I just need to assemble a few last pieces of evidence ... Say, Kenkichi, what's that you're holding?'

I had noticed a white piece of paper in the boy's hand.

'I found it hanging on the door ...'

It was a sign resembling the one we had found yesterday. On it, written with what looked like the same black brush, were the words:

THIRD VICTIM

At first, neither Sawako nor Sonoe seemed to grasp the sign's significance. On the other hand, I immediately understood the implication. The third victim was to be Sawako or Sonoe. And if Akimitsu's suspicions were correct ...

I no longer even had the energy to speak. A strange weariness seemed to have come over my entire body. I slipped wordlessly from the room, made my way to the garden and stood on the bluff where the second murder had taken place.

The sea breeze felt like a balm on my exhausted face. Below me lay the blue, calmly undulating expanse of Tokyo Bay, beyond which I could just make out the low, curving outline of the Chiba mountains. The rippled clouds overhead were limned with gold, red and purple, providing an autumnal contrast to the thunderclouds gathering in front of the setting sun.

The water below me connected Japan to Burma, Malaya and the islands of the South Pacific, and now I found myself thinking of those friends of mine, promising young men all of them, who had lost their lives in the war. They had never desired death or bloodshed; a force bigger than them had simply herded them into that theatre of destruction. All their efforts, all their miserly hopes, turned out to be nothing but a vain and fleeting fantasy in the face of the crushing reality of war. But had their lives—and deaths—really meant nothing? Had they really left no trace in this world?

The clouds came, and the clouds went. At the internment camp where I'd been held in Burma, I'd often gazed at the sky above and dreamed of the mountainous landscape of my homeland. From the deck of the steamboat carrying me back to Japan, I had stared at the sea and thought of Tokyo Bay, to which it was distantly connected. And now here they were—those mountains, that bay—stretching out before my very eyes. But what great changes had been wrought in the hearts of the Japanese in the meantime! In the end, would any of those who hadn't been sent to war ever understand what we went through in those years of savage, life-or-death combat?

My eyes were suddenly drawn to the rocks a few metres below me. In their shade I had noticed what appeared to be an empty syringe. I made my way down and picked it up. The needle was still attached, and I could see no trace of liquid inside. It had been discarded here, quite some distance from where we had discovered Yojiro's body last night. As for the connection between an empty syringe and the murders …

'Koichi!' called a voice from behind me. It was Sawako. She must have followed me here. 'So you're leaving us, then? And not even taking me with you … You really don't care how I feel, do you?'

Her eyes brimmed with resentment. At the same time, with the gentle breeze teasing and tousling her thick black hair, there was something quite bewitching about her slender figure.

I knew I needed to resolve things with her at some point. But this did not feel like the right time.

'I need to get away from this house, Sawako.'

'Where will you go?'

'I haven't decided yet.'

'Koichi, you really don't understand women, do you? Sometimes I wonder if you're even made of flesh and blood. You know that Rintaro rules our family with an iron fist. Nobody has ever been able to stand up to him; my father and grandmother have always fearfully obeyed his every word. And now that I've spoken out in your defence, he's furious with me. But I did so willingly, Koichi. Do you realize what would have happened to you if I hadn't intervened?'

I had never really been able to handle Sawako. She was one of those intelligent women who could see right into a man's heart. I, too, understood how she felt—and yet there was simply nothing I could do. I broke away, leaving her standing there on the bluff. In no time at all, dusk had lowered its dark veil around the grey Chizui mansion.

After dinner, I busied myself in the laboratory. There was still a great deal for me to do, and only a day and a half left in which to do it. At nine, when I'd finished for the day, I retired to my own quarters—a small six-mat room in the cottage that stood just a few metres from the main house. The Japanese-style building was normally reserved for guests—not that the Chizui mansion saw many these days.

I crawled under my mosquito net, but sleep was reluctant to come. *Portia* … *Portia* … the name felt familiar somehow. I knew it to be a Western woman's name—in fact, it was the name of Brutus' wife in Shakespeare's *Julius Caesar*, as well as the female protagonist of his *Merchant of Venice* ...

Just then, I heard the entrance door of the cottage open quietly. Instinctively, I sat up in bed and looked at my clock. It was ten past twelve. Who could be visiting me at this time of night?

Part of me wants to end this journal here—or at the very least, for the sake of Sawako's honour, to omit the episode that follows. But by the following afternoon, Sawako had departed from this world. I believe, therefore, that I have a duty to establish her innocence. For that reason, and no other, I have decided to set down the truth here in writing.

Standing outside my room, then, was Sawako Chizui, dressed in a purple gown and pyjamas.

'What are you doing here?'

'Shh! We can't talk out here. Let me in, won't you?'

Under the dim electric light of the porch, I could clearly make out her brooding features. Silently, I stepped aside.

'Is your grandmother asleep?'

'Yes, she's just taken a sedative. She's fast asleep.'

'Did you lock the room on your way out?'

'No. Why?'

'Well, isn't that a little dangerous?'

'What's the point in worrying any more? We'll all be dead before long, anyway. That's my family's sad fate, Koichi, don't you see?'

In these words, and the way her body slackened as she tried to wrap her arms around me, I sensed a sort of wild and reckless abandon.

'Steady, Sawako ... What if someone sees?'

'I don't care, Koichi. So you're a coward, too? Are you going to make me start this?'

It seemed I was made of flesh and blood, after all. I felt the warmth of her breath, the nearness of her soft, flushed hands. Another five minutes, and I don't dare to think what might have happened. But just then, I was saved by an unexpected sound.

Someone had rapped on one of the shutters. Sawako froze, then clung to me. I silently indicated the closet built into the wall of the room, then immediately hurried out, still in my bedclothes.

Standing there in the darkness was the deranged Hisako, her face as white as a sheet. She must have slipped out of her room somehow. A low noise—half-giggle, half-sob—welled up from somewhere deep in her throat. Her eyes glistened vacantly in the gloom; her face was like a Noh mask, incapable of expressing either sadness or happiness.

'Eighty-eight in eighty-two,' she murmured. 'Eighty-eight in eighty-two.'

I'd never heard Hisako say these words before. And yet they were an exact match for the ones her mother had uttered—the secret phrase she had kept safe in her memory throughout a decade of confinement.

Then it struck me. If Hisako and her mother both knew this phrase, then it seemed likely the Professor had, too. In fact, what if he was the one who taught them it?

Just then, Hisako abruptly spun around and hurried off into the darkness.

'Hisako, be careful!' I cried, running after her. She was nearing the cliff at the end of the garden when I finally managed to restrain her. Then she stopped moving entirely. I held her apparently unconscious body in my arms. From overhead came the fierce squawking of a gull, summoning its companions from somewhere over the sea. Illuminated by the moonlight streaming through the clouds, Hisako's face was blanched and ghostly.

I couldn't leave her here. Still holding her in my arms, I made my way back towards the mansion. The back door was unlocked. Even in the darkness, I was able to find my way down the hall. Just then, one of the maids abruptly slid open the panelled door that led to their room.

I began explaining the situation. 'Hisako got out of the house somehow. I heard something outside the cottage, and when I got up to have a look, there she was. She ran off towards the cliff, but I managed to restrain her. It was quite a close call, really …'

The maid's expression was puzzled. 'I was sure we locked the back door. I wonder how it got open?'

'Maybe someone went out to the garden and forgot to lock it again …'

'Shall I help you with her, sir?'

'No, I'll manage.'

Still cradling Hisako's unconscious body, I made my way upstairs.

'Kenkichi? Are you awake?'

Hearing no reply, I pulled the doorknob towards me and entered the room. The boy was fast asleep, and I didn't want to wake him. I laid Hisako down on the bed gently and pulled a blanket over her. After another ten minutes or so, I made my way back downstairs.

The maid appeared again, still looking concerned. 'Everything okay, sir?'

'I think so. But stay alert!'

'Yes, sir. Goodnight.'

I heard her lock the back door after me and stopped dead in my tracks. How was Sawako going to get back into the house now?

I stood there for a moment, racking my brains. Then I remembered something. When I left the laboratory earlier,

133

one of the windows had been unlatched. If I gave her a boost, she'd probably be able to get in that way. Reassured by this thought, I made my way back to the cottage.

Inside, I found Sawako waiting for me with a worried look on her face. Her earlier passion seemed to have evaporated entirely.

'What happened, Koichi?'

I explained the situation briefly.

'Then what should we do?' she frowned. 'We can't wake the maid ...'

'There's a window off the latch in the laboratory. I'll help you climb through it.'

'Yes, let's do that,' nodded Sawako, springing to her feet. But when she turned back to face me, a note of sadness had crept into her voice. 'Koichi, fate can be a cruel old thing, don't you think? Just like that, our last chance has slipped by. The stars never did align for us, did they ...'

I didn't know what to reply. We were silent as we made our way across the dewy grass, and yet a wordless exchange seemed to take place between us—one that even the wind couldn't catch ...

I gave the laboratory window a push; it swung open easily. Sawako climbed onto my shoulders, then quietly slipped into the dark interior. I lingered there for a moment after she had gone, then gathered myself and returned to the cottage.

I was too agitated to sleep properly. Sinister dreams plagued me through the night. At around five o'clock, I awoke filled with vague apprehension. My bedclothes were soaked through with cold sweat. I quickly took down the mosquito net and folded away my bedding. When I slid the door of the closet to one side, I felt a jolt in my chest.

Someone had opened the trunk where I kept my most precious belongings.

134

I began frantically checking its contents. My money and watch were still there. The only thing missing turned out to be my small six-chambered revolver. It wasn't some souvenir from Burma; in fact, a friend had gifted it to me before I left for the front. But it was quite an antiquated model, and I soon came into possession of a newer type. I had therefore left it in the care of another friend together with some other things and, having only retrieved it a few days ago, had not yet registered it with the authorities.

The thief had to be Sawako. But what could she have wanted my revolver for?

I couldn't just stay there. I quickly got dressed and hurried out of the cottage. A white mist enveloped the mansion; it was an unusually cold morning for summer.

Just then, I noticed a dark figure walking towards me through the mist. As we neared each other, I realized that it was a policeman. I even recognized his face.

'Has something happened, Officer?'

'There was a third murder at the mansion last night.'

'Who?'

'The old lady.'

Sonoe. The third victim had been not Rintaro, nor Sawako, but Sonoe. I took a deep breath, then asked: 'How did she die? Was she shot?'

The policeman gave me a puzzled look.

'Why would you think that? No, it was another heart attack. Happened in her room between midnight and one o'clock last night. They found a Noh costume on the body, apparently— one with a snake-scale pattern.'

By ordering those coffins, the murderer had signalled that there would be three killings. If that were true, the Chizui family murders ought, by now, to have reached their conclusion. And yet something told me we had not yet reached the grand finale. Sonoe's death might have marked the end of the murder case—but in the tragedy of the Chizui family, there were still several appalling acts to come.

8

The Greene Murder Case

The familiar jasmine-like fragrance pervaded the bedroom. Lying on the bed, her face contorted with anguish and surprise, was the frail old body of Sonoe Chizui.

The brocaded Noh costume that had been draped over her lower body reached almost to the floor. I was particularly struck by its snake-scale pattern—the kind worn, in both Noh and Kabuki, by female demons. In other words, just like the spray of maple leaves, this was a prop that the murderer had deliberately left at the scene.

In Van Dine's *The Bishop Murder Case*, the villain uses the Mother Goose nursery rhymes as inspiration for a series of killings. The murderer, to whom humanity, morality and the law have come to mean nothing in the face of the vastness of the cosmos, finds a bizarre attraction in these nursery rhymes. Could this Noh costume indicate a similar sort of sinister playfulness on the part of the murderer?

The police were grilling Sawako in the downstairs reception room. She had an alibi, but would she be able to bring herself to use it?

The murderer must have sneaked into her bedroom while she was visiting me in the cottage. Of course, it was theoretically possible that Sawako was indeed the murderer and had committed the crime either before or after her visit—and yet I just couldn't see her as the culprit. On my own, however, I would be powerless to help her. Seeing no other option, I called Akimitsu and asked for his help. But when he arrived at the mansion fifteen minutes later, he appeared indifferent to her plight.

'I'm telling you, it must have been her,' he said, after ushering me into the study. 'No matter how despicable Rintaro might be as an individual, there's simply no evidence that he's the killer. Whereas Sawako—well, she's clearly the prime suspect.'

'Go on then—prove to me she's the murderer.'

'Very well. Let's start with the telephone calls. Given the location of the phone booth, the only place anyone could eavesdrop from is the hallway. Sawako told us she saw Taijiro making a phone call. But that evening, a total of three phone calls were made from the mansion. First the hotel, then the undertaker and finally the Oka Asylum. Now, we don't know for sure who made each of these calls, but it seems quite evident that it wasn't Taijiro who telephoned the undertaker. No, it must have been the murderer who ordered those coffins.

'Now, what about the call to the Oka Asylum? Again, it seems unlikely that Taijiro made it. Why? Because we know that he made the first call—and if the second was made by the murderer, Taijiro would have needed to return to the booth to make the third. But if you had two phone calls to make, you would normally make them together, wouldn't you? Still, let's imagine that he didn't—that after telephoning us at the hotel, he waited in the hall while the murderer called the undertaker—well, he would have overheard that phone call. In which case, surely he would have told someone about it?

'So, if the first call was made by Taijiro, it seems impossible that he made the second and third calls. In other words, the call he was making when Sawako saw him from the hallway *must* have been the call to the hotel. When she visited me at the hotel and I pressed her about that phone call, she countered by suggesting that Taijiro could have been calling somewhere else. Now, that comment may have helped us discover the truth about the Oka Asylum, but it seems safe to say Taijiro only made one phone call that evening—the one to the hotel.

'And don't forget, Sawako knows shorthand. I found out as much by springing that trap on her. So, tell me: who could have made that transcript, if not her? We still don't know whether she dropped the piece of paper intentionally or by accident—but either way, it was a fatal error.

'It must have been Sawako herself who made the second and third calls. Most likely she entered the phone booth as soon as Taijiro had finished the first call. When she was done, she went upstairs to the spare room, took the Noh mask from its case and went to knock on Taijiro's door. If she's not the murderer, can you really imagine her venturing alone, at night, into the room where that terrifying object was displayed?

'Now we come to the problem of the locked room. I really had to rack my brains over this one. But then I remembered *The Greene Murder Case*, by Van Dine. I'm sure even you must have read that one. I reckon Sawako has too—and assuming she has, the method she used becomes obvious.

'Imagine you were to pass a metal skewer through the hole in the shank of the key, then attach a string to the tip of the skewer. That way, when the key is turned and the door locked, the skewer will slip through the key and onto the floor. You fasten some kind of weight to the other end of the string—a piece of lead, for instance—and leave that dangling from one of the pivot widows. You go outside and pull the weight from below; the door in the room locks; another tug, and the skewer comes tumbling out of the window. All of which would explain why Sawako was so keen to go out to the garden.'

'Very interesting. No wonder you go around calling yourself the Japanese Philo Vance ... But how do you suppose the pivot window was closed afterwards?'

'I'll admit I'm not sure about that part. Of course, from inside the room you'd just need to pull the window cord. From outside, meanwhile, a gentle push would suffice—but from six or seven metres below the window ... I'm not sure what precise method Sawako used. I suppose we'll have to ask her when she confesses.'

'Giving up that easily, are you? But what about the actual murder—how was that done, then?'

'Koichi, there are certain karate techniques which we lay-people know nothing about. Breaking a three-centimetre plank with just three fingers, for example. I imagine there must be a technique like that which could trigger a heart attack.'

'Goodness, Akimitsu, you really are desperate, aren't you! Tell me, do you have any proof for this claim that Sawako is a karate expert?'

'I imagine she'll confess that part, too.'

'This really isn't like you, Akimitsu. It's not just your approach that is entirely illogical—you're surprisingly short on convincing ideas, too.'

'Well, there's never been a murder like this in any of the novels I've read.'

'You know, I think you've crammed so much knowledge into that brain of yours that you've completely lost sight of how to actually apply it. How about setting your novels to one side for a moment? After all, as a philosopher once put it, true creativity begins with forgetting everything you know. Anyway, what about that jasmine fragrance?'

'I imagine Sawako couldn't bear to just leave the victims as they were, so she decided to add a feminine, romantic touch. A sort of embellishment, as it were. The Noh mask, the maple leaves and the costume were all intended to have a similar decorative effect.'

'I have a rather different explanation for the mask, though I suppose you might be right about the leaves and the costume. But how do you explain that scream we heard?'

'You must have spotted the gramophone by the piano in the spare room. It would be easy enough to conceal it with a blanket or something, then play a recording of a scream. Another trick of Van Dine's.'

I was reaching the end of my tether. It appeared Akimitsu's talents were better suited to literary analysis than solving crimes. All he seemed capable of was dredging up vaguely similar situations from the books he'd read and somehow connecting them to the one at hand. I imagine that the murderer would have been similarly amused to hear him carry on like this. Still, oblivious to my growing frustration, he continued his long-winded explanation.

'With the second murder, the only person who could have persuaded Yojiro out into the garden an hour earlier than planned was Sawako, who was in the dining room with him at that time. And the only person who we know was near the gazebo at nine twenty-six was—once again—Sawako.

'It's the same with the third murder. She was the only other person sleeping in that room. Whatever she might claim, she's clearly the prime suspect.'

By now I'd lost all faith in Akimitsu's abilities. Clearly, his stubborn preconceptions had got the better of him, and I could no longer count on his assistance. Ever since that phone call, he had become immersed in his own wild theories, fully believing himself to be some kind of genius. There was nothing for it, I thought to myself. I'd have to solve the murders on my own.

'Tell me, Akimitsu—what do you think her motive was?'

Just then, there was a knock at the door. It was Mr Ishikari, carrying a briefcase – though for a moment I barely recognized him. His eyes and cheeks had sunk; his face was haggard and lined with worry. It was as though he'd aged ten years overnight.

'Morning, gentlemen.' He seated himself in an armchair and stared absent-mindedly at the books lining the walls. Caught in a shaft of fresh sunlight, his face appeared even paler. 'Thank you both again for yesterday.'

'How did Sawako's interrogation go?' asked Akimitsu impatiently. But when Mr Ishikari replied, it was in a weary voice.

'I can't comment on that in an official capacity. Still, considering how helpful you've both been, I'll tell you what I can off the record. Sawako's in an even more vulnerable position than you two realize.'

'What do you mean by that?'

'We've confirmed the truth about her parenthood.'

Another shudder ran through me. A new page of the Chizui family secret was being revealed before our eyes—and yet all I felt was apprehension.

Mr Ishikari produced a notebook from his briefcase and began flicking through it.

'You've probably been wondering what on earth the police have been doing over the past three days. Don't worry—they haven't just been twiddling their thumbs.

'They obtained a statement from a woman named Tsuru Matsuno, who once served in Taijiro Chizui's household. She was very close to the now-deceased Mrs Chizui—Taijiro's wife, that is—and for a long time oversaw the smooth running of the house. Her statement has provided firm evidence for what Doctor Yamamoto suggested yesterday. She's quite an elderly lady and her statement is a little muddled in places, but I'll try to summarize briefly.

'Mrs Matsuno worked for Taijiro's family from 1913 until the autumn of 1928, during which time, as you know, Rintaro, Yojiro and Sawako were born. Yesterday, Doctor Yamamoto alerted us to the fact that Sawako couldn't be Taijiro's biological child, but it seems the police had already twigged this might be the case. In those days Taijiro was doing rather well for himself as a private doctor, and usually had additional maids in his service, but it was Mrs Matsuno his wife trusted the most, consulting her about even the most private matters. Knowing all this, the police decided to tap her for the truth about Sawako.

'At first Mrs Matsuno remained tight-lipped. Unwilling to betray Mrs Chizui's confidence and honour, she seemed intent on taking the family's secret to the grave—but eventually she had a change of heart. After who knows how many rounds of questioning, she broke down in tears and confessed the truth.

'A year before Sawako was born, Mrs Chizui began suffering from mild pleurisy, and relocated with Yojiro to a fishing village not far from Zushi for convalescence. Mrs Matsuno went with her as her maid and nurse; Taijiro himself visited once a week. Gradually, Mrs Chizui's condition began to improve. Then, one autumn day, she had a chance encounter with the man she had loved in her youth. Now, to most men, such youthful dalliances are like a sprig of wild chrysanthemum, broken off on a whim as they pass and just as immediately discarded. The names of those first loves—sometimes even their order of appearance—are easily forgotten. But to women, love is a more vital force—and they never forget the person who first kindled its fire in their breast.

'He was a down-and-out painter—a man of prodigious talent and unbounded passion who, ground down by adversity, had failed to keep up with the style of the times. He led a life of penury before eventually committing suicide, and it was only after his death that the true value of his work was recognized. But when he was still a penniless art student, he and the young Mrs Chizui had embarked on a passionate romance.

'However, Mrs Chizui's family were too pragmatically minded to give the match their blessing. An eccentric painter with no reputation to speak of—there was no way that her family, industrialists of good social standing, would allow the relationship to go ahead. And so the two were painfully wrenched apart. Eventually, Mrs Chizui resigned herself to her life of marriage to Taijiro, and the months and years went by. I'm sure you can imagine the turbulent emotions that were aroused when they bumped into each other again after all that time.

'Mrs Chizui never revealed exactly how far the relationship went. But after she gave birth to Sawako, Mrs Matsuno watched with secret trepidation as, over the years, the child's face gradually came to resemble that of the painter. Taijiro didn't notice anything at first, but when Sawako was four or five, an unrelated blood test happened to reveal the secret. From then on, he and his wife lived almost entirely apart.

'Shortly afterwards, Mrs Matsuno took her leave of the family; not long after that, Mrs Chizui died from an illness. Sawako was left alone in the world. As she grew older, she began to have her own doubts about her parentage. One day, she visited Mrs Matsuno's house and managed to squeeze the truth from her. After revealing the secret, the old maid told her: "Sawako, you must see that your mother is partly to blame for all this. In any case, what matters most is who raised you. Never forget everything you owe your father."

'"Don't worry. I understand that much," replied Sawako firmly. But Mrs Matsuno tells us that as she gazed off into space, her eyes glistened with tears.

'That, in brief, was the old woman's statement. Maybe it's little more than an anecdote, with no direct relevance to the investigation. But if Sawako is indeed the murderer, it certainly provides a clue as to her motive. All those years of harsh treatment and pressure ... if Taijiro had been her real father, perhaps she would have accepted that as her lot. But once she discovered the truth about her birth, that acceptance must have curdled into an overwhelming feeling of injustice—leading, finally, to an eruption of rage ...'

Mr Ishikari lowered his eyes as if in sympathy, his gaze eventually coming to rest on a carving of a nymph above the fireplace.

At this point, the door opened and Inspector Yoshino walked in. His pale, clean-shaven face bore no hint of fatigue or anxiety.

'Ah, Mr Ishikari, here you are. We need your signature on Sawako Chizui's arrest warrant.'

Mr Ishikari nodded gravely. But as he picked up his fountain pen, something deep inside me impelled me to act.

'Wait!' I cried. 'Sawako isn't the murderer. If you'll just give me a little time, I can prove who was really behind all this.'

The three of them froze completely, like a film stuck in the projector: Mr Ishikari raising his pen, Akimitsu readying his lighter and Yoshino laying the warrant on the desk. In that brief silence—the calm before the storm—I could almost hear the fanfare of a bugle sounding my advance.

'Koichi, do you really think you know who did it?' asked Mr Ishikari in a quiet voice.

'I do. In fact, I'm absolutely certain. Please—will you listen to what I have to say?'

'All right. But make it brief,' replied Yoshino, before taking a seat. And so, with the trio's piercing gaze upon me, I began to explain.

'Let me begin by proving that Sawako is innocent. I'm assuming it was last night's murder in particular that convinced you of her guilt. Now, did she tell you where she was last night between the hours of midnight and one o'clock?'

'She was crying too much to get an answer out of her, but we can assume she was in her bedroom. Anyway, if she didn't commit the crime, is it really plausible for her not to have noticed when someone came into the room and murdered the old woman sleeping next to her?'

'Inspector, I can assure you that Sawako was not in her room at that time.'

My three listeners appeared dumbfounded. Yoshino was glaring at me so vehemently that I worried his eyeballs might pop out from their sockets.

'But … how would you know that?' he asked.

'Because she was in my room instead.'

'Mr Yanagi,' said Yoshino, his voice growing hoarse, 'forgive me for asking, but are you and Sawako … romantically involved?'

'No—and in the end, nothing inappropriate happened last night, either. You see, at around ten past midnight, Sawako knocked on the door of my cottage. Now, I don't doubt that she feels more than friendly affection towards me; nor would it be true for me to say I am entirely blind to her charms. But human relationships depend on more than mutual fondness.

And, until then, ours had never exceeded the bounds of friendship.

'Since yesterday, I have begun to take a more active role in the investigation—a fact that appears to have aggravated the surviving members of the Chizui family. I have therefore made it clear that I intend to leave this house tomorrow. That must have been what compelled Sawako to throw caution to the wind and visit me in the middle of the night like that. I suppose she thought it was her last chance to confess her feelings.

'It turned out, however, there was no time for anything at all. We heard someone pounding on the shutters outside; for some reason, Hisako had come rushing out of the house. I ran after her and managed to restrain her on the bluff, at which point she fainted. I carried her unconscious body back into the house through the rear entrance. The maid was awake and will be able to confirm that the back door was unlocked at that time.

'I went up to Hisako's room, laid her on her bed and returned through the back door to my cottage. I then realized that the maid had locked the door behind me. Worrying about how Sawako was going to get inside again, I remembered that one of the windows in the laboratory was open. I helped Sawako in through that window. It must have been at least forty minutes after midnight by then.

'Sawako was therefore absent from her bedroom for over half an hour. I think you will agree that it is at least possible that the murderer slipped into the bedroom while she was gone?'

Nobody spoke; not even a cough broke the silence. I carried on.

'Now, let us consider the first murder. Earlier, Akimitsu outlined a possible method by which Taijiro's room might have been sealed, but I'm afraid I didn't find his theory convincing in the slightest. However, a more plausible method has occurred to me. Gentlemen, the door to that room was locked from a quite unexpected location. In a moment, I'll conduct a little experiment to show you what I mean—and establish, beyond a doubt, the real perpetrator of the crime. Akimitsu here has argued that the sequence of the phone calls proved that Sawako had to be the murderer, but I have a rather different interpretation.'

Just then, the maid called for Akimitsu. He was wanted on the telephone. When he returned after a brief absence, he wore an oddly melancholy expression. In the meantime, Yoshino had got the maid to confirm what I'd said about the back door being unlocked. Now, seated opposite me, the inspector stared at me in stubborn silence.

'Inspector, what time was the body discovered this morning?' I asked.

'Just before five o'clock, I believe. Sawako claims she awoke at dawn and noticed that her grandmother had been covered from the waist up with the old brocaded Noh costume that was normally kept in a chest of drawers in the room. Finding this rather strange, she pulled it off her grandmother—and was suddenly overpowered by the sweet smell of jasmine. Sonoe was dead—and from another heart attack.'

I didn't need to hear any more. I sprang to my feet.

'There's something I want to ask Sawako. Would that be possible?'

'Well, yes, I suppose.' Yoshino seemed almost intimidated.

But as I strode towards the door, Akimitsu stopped me.

'Koichi, a quick word?'

He took me to a corner of the study and began speaking in a low voice.

'It appears I was mistaken. I fully retract my accusation against Sawako. I am very intrigued as to how you intend to reveal the murderer's identity, but as it happens I've just been called away on an urgent personal matter. I must return to Tokyo at once. I'm leaving this case in your capable hands.

'Koichi, I have no doubt that you will solve the mystery of this affair. Now, here's that transcript of the telephone conversation. I'm entrusting it to you. Use it when you see fit; it will be your secret weapon. I'll leave the exact timing up to you.'

Akimitsu handed me a folder containing the transcript. I thanked him deeply, wished him well, then whispered one last request in his ear.

He stared at me in surprise. 'And what would you need *that* for?'

'It's a vital part of my plan. I intend to use the same trick you used at the hotel.'

Akimitsu retrieved a notepad from his bag and wrote out a phrase in shorthand before handing the note to me. I took it and held out a hand for him to shake. After a moment's hesitation, he grasped it firmly and said quietly:

'I wish you well, Koichi. Farewells are difficult. You know, ever since the war, I've begun to feel that life can be rather cruel. After finally being reunited after all these years, we're parting again. I don't know when or where we'll meet next, but please—do take good care of yourself.'

I felt my cheeks growing warm. In each other's company we had been quick to bicker and squabble, but now that he was leaving I felt a wave of sadness. I might have my doubts about his ability and character, but I could only feel deep gratitude for the friendship he had shown me.

Against the dark backdrop of infinite space and time, our short lives are nothing but a momentary spark, a firefly's glimmer—emerging from eternity only to disappear back into it. And friendships we thought would last forever can fade in the flicker of a shooting star ...

While I stood there grappling with my emotions, Akimitsu made his way over to Mr Ishikari.

'Prosecutor, I'm afraid I must return to Tokyo on urgent personal business. Thank you very much for everything; we have been lucky to have you. Now, there's a private matter I'd like to discuss—would you be able to join me in the garden?'

Mr Ishikari seemed somewhat hesitant.

'I'm sorry to hear that. But this discussion of yours ... can't it wait?'

'I really am in a hurry. I'd appreciate it if we could talk now.'

'Well, can't we talk here?'

'I'm afraid that's no good.'

'Very well. If you insist ... Inspector Yoshino, don't start on Sawako again until I get back, okay?'

He and Akimitsu disappeared quietly off down the hall. I sat down again, my mind awhirl. Five minutes went by, and then ten, and still Mr Ishikari did not return. I took a deep breath, then turned to Yoshino.

'Have you questioned Rintaro yet?'

'Yes, we've done an initial interrogation. We'll grill him again if necessary, though.'

'Please do. Show him this piece of paper, and watch how he reacts.'

I gave him the note Akimitsu had just written out for me.

'Is this Korean?' he asked, squinting in confusion. 'Hieroglyphics, maybe? Some kind of cipher?'

'It's Nakane shorthand. It's Japanese all right—just written differently.'

'I see. And ... which way up does it go?'

150

'This way, I believe.'

'But what does it say?'

'I can't tell you that just yet … Ah, Mr Ishikari. Are you all right?'

Mr Ishikari was standing in the doorway, as pale as if he'd seen a ghost. He tottered unsteadily over to the bookshelf and leaned against it.

'Feeling unwell, sir?' said Yoshino, rushing over to support him. 'Perhaps you should take a seat …'

'Oh, it's nothing—just a spot of dizziness. Could you get me some water?'

Yoshino quickly fetched a glass of water from the dining room. Mr Ishikari drank the whole thing in one gulp, sank into an armchair and closed his eyes. His breathing was ragged; sweat trickled down his forehead. What on earth could have put him in this state?

A few minutes later, when Mr Ishikari had gathered himself, we made our way to the reception room downstairs where Sawako was being questioned. She looked up in alarm as she heard us approaching. There wasn't a trace of make-up on her tear-streaked face; dark rings had formed below her eyes, her hair was dishevelled, her expression strangely deadened. The white roses displayed on a small table behind her seemed, by contrast, to flaunt their pointless beauty; I found my gaze drifting to them to avoid having to reckon with the pitiful woman in front of them.

Yoshino began the interrogation in a low voice:

'Miss Sawako, you lied to us, didn't you? You went somewhere between midnight and one o'clock last night, didn't you?'

'I went nowhere at all,' said Sawako in a spiteful, broken voice.

'Are you sure about that? You have a sympathetic audience here. I know this must be hard for you to talk about, but Koichi

151

has told us something that, if true, would put you in a much safer position. If you could just confirm it for us, the suspicion against you will lessen considerably, if not entirely. So please, Miss Sawako—won't you tell us where you were?'

She didn't even attempt to reply. I decided to intervene.

'Sawako, I know what you're thinking. You want to maintain your honour even if it means putting your own life at risk. Yes, I told these two the truth about last night, but I did so with only one aim in mind: keeping you from harm. It's not as though anything actually happened between us, and whatever you say will never leave this room. Please, do this for me. Tell us the truth, and help us unmask the murderer.'

She flicked her eyes up at me, but now, rather than glistening with tears, they seemed to smoulder with rage. I found myself getting to my feet.

'Koichi, there are some secrets a woman can never tell— even if it means carrying them to the grave. I cannot speak of what happened last night, nor shall you ever hear the name of the murderer from these lips.' Her voice shook bitterly, then rose to a shriek. 'Koichi … I want you to die with me!'

She produced my revolver—where had she hidden it?—and levelled it at my chest. There was a loud crack as I flung myself to the floor. The bullet had grazed my right arm and passed through the window behind me.

With horrified expressions, Yoshino and the police guards sprang towards Sawako. But it was too late.

She had sent the second bullet straight into her own chest. A crimson flower bloomed abruptly on her white blouse. She stumbled backwards, then, murmuring something, fell against the small table behind her. As she crumpled to the floor, the white roses tumbled from their vase and onto her lifeless body. Soon they, too, had been dyed a deep red. One petal at a time, they seemed to mourn the passing of this beautiful and ill-fated woman.

We could barely move. It was an absurd thing to have happened in broad daylight; it seemed more like a scene from some strange dream.

'But,' I blurted, finally breaking the silence, 'she really wasn't the murderer.'

'Indeed. She really wasn't,' came a voice from the doorway, scornfully echoing my own. I spun around. Standing there in his black gown and pyjamas, blowing a cloud of cigarette smoke in our direction, was Rintaro Chizui.

9

The Merchant of Venice

(Koichi Yanagi's journal, continued)

With Sawako's abrupt suicide, the Chizui family tragedy had taken an unexpected turn—one that even I had failed to foresee.

She had loved me, and I had been unable to accept that love. She had known who the real murderer was, but she had chosen to take that secret to her grave. I could think of various possible motives for her doing so, but the truth is that a woman's feelings are not so easily unravelled. Even when she was pointing the gun at my own chest, I had felt neither anger nor fear towards her. Instead, it was as though I glimpsed, for a brief instant, the abyss that lurks beneath the surface of all of our lives.

Freed from love, hatred and suffering, her spirit had departed for the celestial realm. I knelt by the beautiful body she had left behind and joined my palms together in prayer. With no incense to offer her, I took the remaining white roses and silently laid them on her bloodied chest. Then, with a concerted effort, I tore myself away from the room.

What had Rintaro meant by those scornful words? Did he, too, know who was behind the killings? He had boasted that he would reveal the murderer at one o'clock tomorrow afternoon. But what was the ace he thought he had up his sleeve … ?

Still, I was confident I was a step ahead. I had already solved the mystery of the locked room. Only one puzzle remained: the words that Kayoko had uttered on her deathbed.

I returned to the study, where Mr Ishikari and Inspector Yoshino were waiting.

'That was a close call, Koichi,' said Mr Ishikari in a consoling tone. 'I'm just glad you're unharmed.'

'Sir,' said Yoshino, 'I owe you an apology. We had no idea she might be carrying a revolver … If we'd been able to take her into custody and really put the screws on her, I reckon she'd have given us the name of the murderer.'

'I wouldn't be so sure, Inspector. After all, she was ready to take her own life rather than betray the secret. You could have poured hot lead on her and she probably still wouldn't have cracked. No, this was no blunder of yours. Anyway, Koichi, you mentioned you have a theory as to the murderer's identity. Perhaps we should hear it?'

But I was barely conscious of Mr Ishikari's words. *Hot lead*—these words had provided the spark I'd needed all this time. Hot lead. The lead on the Noh mask. The unexpected lightness of the lead in the laboratory. Eighty-eight in eighty-two. Portia. *The Merchant of Venice.*

I had finally penetrated the mystery. Why had it taken me so long to join up the dots? I stood and went to stare at the words that were framed on the wall.

> All that glisters is not gold;
> Often have you heard that told:
> Some there be that shadows kiss;
> Such have but a shadow's bliss;
> You that choose not by the view,
> Chance as fair and choose as true!

I repeated the words over and over. Before I knew it, a laugh had risen uncontrollably in my throat. At the same time, my eyes grew hot with tears.

'What is it, Koichi?' asked Yoshino, grasping me by the shoulders. He looked concerned; perhaps he thought I'd gone mad from all the excitement. But no: I was completely sane. The answer had finally revealed itself to me.

'Mr Ishikari, this is it. Here!' I cried, pointing at the words in the frame. '*This* is the Professor's will.'

He stared at me in bafflement. 'That bit of English verse? What on earth do you mean?'

'Don't you see? These are some of the most famous lines from *The Merchant of Venice*. And the name that Kayoko uttered on her deathbed, Portia—why, that's the heroine from the same play!'

He finally seemed to have grasped what I was getting at. He rose from his chair and came over to join me.

'The Professor's will … *The Merchant of Venice* … Koichi, how does it all connect? Tell me at once. I must know.'

I sat back down in my chair, dabbed at the sweat on my forehead with a handkerchief and carefully began to explain.

'When you mentioned hot lead just now, it gave me a huge jolt. Those words provided the last link in the chain. I'm sure you remember Kayoko's last utterances: "Eighty-eight in eighty-two", and "Portia". Were those really only the delirious ravings of a dying woman? She died before we could establish whether or not she'd really been sane all along. But if I could just find some kind of meaning in those words of hers, that would be all the proof I needed. Now, finally, I've found that proof.

'Last night, when I found Hisako outside my cottage, she blurted something out. It was the very same phrase:

"Eighty-eight in eighty-two". Are we to dismiss that as mere coincidence? Of course not. Throughout her long decade of confinement, Kayoko had guarded these two phrases with every fibre of her being. Why? Because they were the key to the Chizui tragedy.

'Given that both Hisako and Kayoko knew this cryptic phrase, would it be too much of a stretch to imagine they had both learned it from Soichiro? I don't think so. In fact, I'm certain it was the Professor who devised the code.

'A family tearing itself apart over a hidden treasure: it is a tale as old as time. Indeed, as long as greed lingers in human hearts, these lamentable incidents will continue to litter our history; the tragedy of the Chizui family is merely a particularly shocking example. It was Yojiro who revealed to us that Soichiro, worried about the effects of war on the economy, had converted most of his fortune into a valuable object of some kind, which he had then carefully hidden. Yojiro speculated that this treasure was the sole motivating factor behind his father's murder and the two that threatened to follow; I have to say I'm not convinced. But it does seem like a plausible motive for the real opening act of this tragedy: the events of ten years ago.

'Taijiro was an astonishingly greedy man, one who would do anything for the sake of wealth. The lure of a hidden family treasure worth tens of millions of yen was hard for him to resist. Still, I do not think the plot itself was his invention. No, Taijiro simply went along with someone else's plan.

'Yojiro and Sonoe, our other two murder victims, were in on the plot too. Sonoe revealed as much yesterday when she was rambling in her sleep. Sawako and Kenkichi were both in the room at the time. Sawako may no longer be with us, but I'm sure Kenkichi will confirm the old woman's words.

157

'The Professor's mysterious death ten years ago happened in the wake of an explosion in the laboratory—caused, it seems plausible to believe, by someone intentionally leaving ether in a glass flask. The Professor incurred a serious injury, and then, while recovering, died from an unexplained heart attack—just like the victims of the more recent murders. Everything about his death suggests foul play. There's no doubt about it: the Professor died at the hands of Taijiro's family.

'Still, they must have been surprised when they found out just how little they stood to inherit from the Professor. There has to be more, they told themselves. But only the Professor's wife knew its whereabouts. And so they decided to have her committed to a mental asylum indefinitely, in the hope of extracting the secret.

'In this way, their crime remained buried, escaping notice— and the law—for an entire decade. But in the end, there was no escaping the much harsher judgement of heaven. That, gentlemen, is the truth behind the second part of the tragedy: the murders of the past few days.

'But before discussing those, let me show you something that will prove what I have so far only hypothesized: let me reveal the location of the hidden treasure. Tell me, are you familiar with *The Merchant of Venice*? There are two main strands to the plot of Shakespeare's masterpiece. One concerns the famous "pound of flesh" scene in the courthouse; the other is the quest to find a suitor worthy of Portia. Let us focus on the latter. Portia's father dies, leaving behind three caskets as a trial for his daughter's suitors. One made of gold, one silver—and the other mere lead. As Portia reaches adulthood, numerous suitors, drawn by her beauty and enormous fortune, line up to woo her. One after the other, they fail the test that her father had set them, and depart empty-handed.

'Now, what did the gold casket contain? A scroll that begins: *All that glisters is not gold; Often have you heard that told*, accompanied simply by a skull staring vacantly into space. The Prince of Morocco, who chose the casket in question, makes a crestfallen departure from Portia's estate.

'Next is the silver casket, which is found to contain only a poem that includes the lines: *Some there be that shadows kiss; Such have but a shadow's bliss*, together with the portrait of a "blinking idiot". Fate has not smiled on the Prince of Arragon either.

'Finally, we come to the shabby lead casket. Inside are the words: *You that choose not by the view, Chance as fair and choose as true!*—together with an exquisite portrait of Portia. Bassanio realizes that he has triumphed. He wins the hand of the beautiful Portia—together with her massive fortune.

'I am not quoting Shakespeare for the fun of it. Professor Chizui was a world-leading scientist. And any chemist worth their salt knows that there is something even more important, from a scientific perspective, than the Latin alphabet. The whole universe—the entirety of creation, without exception—is formed from just over ninety elements and their compounds. Those elements can be arranged in a sequence based on their atomic number—starting with hydrogen, which has an atomic number of one. Now, the atomic number of lead happens to be eighty-two.'

Mr Ishikari and Yoshino were staring at me in blank amazement. This might be unknown territory for them, but the code was simple enough that any scientist would understand it.

'When Akimitsu and I investigated the laboratory, he picked up the block of lead and commented that it seemed oddly light. With pure metal, there should be no significant variation in relative weight. In which case, there is only one explanation:

the block of lead—"eighty-two", that is—is hollow. And inside it, I believe we will find "eighty-eight". Well, gentlemen, shall we find out if I'm right?'

I got up and made for the door.

'But, Koichi,' came Mr Ishikari's strained voice from behind me, 'which element has the atomic number eighty-eight?'

'Radium. Which, as it happens, is commonly stored in a lead container due to the dangerous radiation it emits. The Professor was a world authority on radiochemistry, so it doesn't completely surprise me that he chose to convert his entire fortune to a few grams of radium, and hide them inside a block of lead.'

My voice was calm. Yes, a few grams of radium—that was the true form of the Chizui family's hidden fortune.

I went into the laboratory, took the chunk of lead from its jar and carefully pierced it with a knife. Sure enough, it was hollow. Inside, we could glimpse the rich lustre of metallic radium. For a moment, Mr Ishikari, Inspector Yoshino and I simply stood there in silence.

The Professor had been murdered and his wife committed to a mental asylum for a decade—and all for the sake of a lump of metal no bigger than a fingertip. Eighty-eight in eighty-two: the hidden cause of the Chizui family's downfall.

'Give this to the police for safe keeping,' I said, sealing the lead again and handing it to Yoshino. 'It'll be dangerous to keep it in this house.'

Mr Ishikari turned to me with a puzzled expression. 'You sure about that, Koichi?'

'Absolutely. For the time being, I want it as far away from here as possible.'

'Understood,' said Yoshino, carefully tucking the block of lead under his arm. I glanced at them both before continuing.

'Well, so much for the family fortune. Now it's time I revealed how the murders were carried out—but it'll be easier to do that at the scene of the crime. Would you mind going upstairs and waiting in Kenkichi and Hisako's room while I get a few things ready here? You could get him to corroborate a few things while you're there. He should be able to confirm everything I've told you.'

'Yoshino, give the radium to one of the other officers and head on upstairs, would you? I'll come up with Koichi.' As Mr Ishikari spoke, he began energetically rummaging through the chemical cabinet.

My own preparations didn't take long. I gathered the items I'd prepared earlier, placed them in a large box, then indicated to Mr Ishikari that I was ready. But he shook his head.

'I'd like to check a few more things here. Please, you go ahead.'

This seemed a little odd to me, but I did as he suggested. I went into the neighbouring study, retrieved the folder containing the shorthand transcript Akimitsu had given me, made a few final preparations, then left the room.

Mr Ishikari still hadn't arrived in the siblings' room. Hisako was fast asleep on her bed, her breath faintly audible, as if she'd forgotten all about the excitement of the previous evening. Had the grisly events of the previous three days cast not even a ripple on the strange, smooth waters of her crazed mind? Once again, I felt tears welling in my eyes.

'Well, Kenkichi has confirmed everything you told us—including Sonoe's delirious confession yesterday,' said Yoshino. 'These people really are monsters, aren't they?'

He seemed almost lost for words. Meanwhile Kenkichi, sitting on a chair in front of him, stared at me solemnly, his face ghastly pale. His brief conversation with Yoshino appeared to have left him quite breathless; he clutched his chest as if in agony. His illness seemed to be increasingly taking its toll; surely his days were now numbered. When the Chizuis had first taken me in, he had been oblivious to his condition, and still earnestly studying for his middle-school entrance examination. Now he seemed to have realized that his life was slowly slipping away. For the one person who might have inherited the Professor's genius to perish so young ... I could barely even contemplate the thought.

But I had come here for other reasons. Another piece of evidence was waiting in this room.

Mr Ishikari opened the door and walked in. His expression seemed racked with some complex, inexpressible emotion, but there was no time for me to worry about what it might be.

'Mr Ishikari,' I began, 'look at these diaries. Akimitsu noticed something odd about them, too. Of course, it's only natural that Hisako hasn't kept a diary in the five years since she went insane. But what about the missing pages in the earlier diaries—the ones she kept seven and ten years ago? It wouldn't make sense for her to tear pages from her own diary. No, someone else must have done this—someone who couldn't stand the idea of anyone else reading these passages. Why? Because in them, his evil deeds were exposed for all to see.

'Now, most people keep their diaries somewhere safe from prying eyes. These days, Hisako is something of a special case, but we can assume that, until the onset of her madness, she kept hers carefully hidden. Someone in this family felt it necessary to remove certain incriminating sections. Who do you think it was?

'In the darkroom in the attic, I discovered a nude photo of Hisako—one so indecent I wanted to cover my eyes. To photograph a woman like that—not some prostitute or professional model, but your own flesh and blood—would require a quite abnormal mental disposition. It would also be impossible if your relationship with her was an ordinary, familial one.

'Yesterday, Doctor Yamamoto pointed us to the root cause of Hisako's insanity. His conclusion was that she had been infected with a malignant disease before undergoing a psychological shock severe enough to induce mental derangement. There is only one other person in the Chizui family who carries the disease in question. Gentlemen, I'm sure you have grasped my meaning.

'Next, let me show you a most mysterious poem—one that, it turns out, reveals the truth behind the heart attacks in both the recent deaths and that of the Professor ten years ago. Take a look.'

I opened the diary and showed Mr Ishikari and Yoshino the poem entitled 'The Mirage'. Mr Ishikari read the poem aloud in a low voice, but didn't seem to see what I was getting at.

'Koichi, this is all a little puzzling. Are you saying there's some hidden meaning to the poem?'

'Don't you see? A poem conveys a single stream of consciousness, and this one is no exception. But there's one part that seems to interrupt the flow. Look at the third stanza— don't you think the language is a little strange?

The faint scent of flowers distracts me from the sky above;
My heart is pierced by an empty gust of wind.

'The three murders were all accompanied by the flowery scent of jasmine. And in each of them, a heart was indeed "pierced". In fact, it was made to stop beating.'

Mr Ishikari and Yoshino were staring at me ashen-faced. Murders carried out in accordance with a poem—it was a crime that recalled the killer's use of the Mother Goose nursery rhymes in *The Bishop Murder Case*.

Mr Ishikari turned to me.

'Koichi,' he said sharply, 'are you saying you know how those heart attacks were caused?'

'I am. Gentlemen, this method will surprise even you—it requires no drugs, no poison and no special technique. Indeed, it's so simple practically anyone could do it.'

'Well, what was it?'

'Recall how, in the first murder, a Noh mask was found on the floor of the locked room. At first I thought it must have been a psychological shock that caused Taijiro's heart attack. But in the second and third murders, there was no indication that the killer had approached the victims wearing the mask. Instead there were only that spray of maple leaves and the snake-scale costume—neither of which seemed sufficient to trigger some death-inducing shock. The murderer must have used a more reliable method. I was utterly perplexed.

'Then, yesterday, I happened to discover an empty syringe not far from the gazebo where the second murder took place. It had a needle attached, but inside there was no trace of any drug.

'But if the syringe had been used to inject some kind of poison, it seems unlikely that the murderer would have simply thrown it away. In a place like that, and with the murder committed within such a brief window of time, there would have been no time to clean the syringe afterwards. Throwing it away meant accepting the possibility that it would be found at some point. And if poison was then detected in the syringe, that might scupper the planned third murder. Therefore, if this syringe was indeed the murder weapon, the logical conclusion is that no poison was used in these killings.

'In that case, what *was* involved? Let's return to that poem. "My heart is pierced", it says—and by what? An "empty gust of wind".

'Gentlemen, I'm sure you've both received an injection at some point. As you'll know, there are two main types—intravenous or hypodermic. With both, you must have noticed how, after drawing the medicine into the syringe, the doctor points the needle upwards and gives it a quick squirt. It becomes such a reflex for the doctor that the actual reason behind it is often forgotten.

'You see, when a doctor fills the syringe, an air bubble naturally forms inside; the purpose of the squirting is to expel that air. But what happens if you forget to do so, and end up injecting it into the bloodstream? With a hypodermic injection it might hurt a little, but no harm will be done. But with an intravenous injection, the effects can be terrifying. Once the air bubble enters the blood, it circulates around the body before eventually reaching the heart. Now, our hearts are really nothing more than extremely delicate pumps. As soon as the air bubble gets inside that pump, it begins to falter. And if the quantity of air is too great, the result is a heart attack. So, if you wanted to murder someone this way, all you'd need to do is inject a large amount of air into one of your victim's veins.

'It really is a quite terrifying method—a crime with no precedent, in fact. Poison, no matter how effective, can always be detected—not to mention the fact that suitable poisons are quite difficult for the ordinary criminal to obtain. By comparison, injecting someone with air is incredibly simple. Not only that, but it leaves no trace of homicidal intent. The entry wound from a needle is so tiny that it is likely to go unnoticed. Who is even to say it was murder?

165

'Gentlemen, do you see? That "gust of wind" was a current of air—one which "pierced" the victim's heart.'

Mr Ishikari and Yoshino appeared horrified. Clearly, a method of murder this simple and effective—not to mention terrifying—had been beyond their imagination.

'But, Mr Yanagi,' said Yoshino with a gulp, 'what was the perfume for?'

'The poem answers that question, too. Look: *The faint scent of flowers distracts me from the sky above.* In other words, the jasmine was a distraction.'

'What do you mean by that?'

'This murder technique is almost perfect, but it has one conspicuous flaw. During the few minutes required for the air bubble to have its deadly effects, the victim must not move an inch—and yet they're hardly going to sit still and let you administer an injection! In which case, what do you suppose the simplest solution would be?'

Inspector Yoshino and Mr Ishikari simply stared at me.

'Isn't it obvious? You use an anaesthetic. The victim only needs to be out cold for a few minutes. The most effective substance for such a purpose would be ether. The murderer subdued his victims that way, then used the injection method to carry out the murder. You'd only need a tiny amount of ether; it probably wouldn't even show up in an autopsy. But it does have a distinctive smell, one that would linger at the scene of the crime. And so the murderer concealed it by sprinkling his victims with a jasmine-scented perfume ...'

'But what about the reference to the sky?'

'Look up the English word "ether" in the dictionary. You'll see it has another, more poetic meaning: the open sky. The jasmine was used to "distract" us from that "sky"—in other words, the smell of the ether.'

By now the two men were grimacing in horror. The awful truth behind the murders had reduced them to silence. All the earlier talk of evil spirits and cursed masks seemed to pale in comparison to this appalling scientific reality.

'Soichiro Chizui was murdered ten years ago using the same method—I'm sure of it. The Professor's heart was healthy; it simply doesn't make sense for him to have suddenly had a heart attack. It seems very likely that ether was involved that time, too—remember the explosion of the glass flask. Now, a decade later, ether and air have once again performed their rhapsody of death in the Chizui family.

'Ten years ago, it wasn't just the Professor, his wife and children staying at this mansion, but also three members of the branch family: Taijiro, Rintaro and Yojiro. Of those three, two have now also died from heart attacks.

'Can that really be written off as simple coincidence? Hardly. I'm convinced that both parts of this tragedy were the work of a single person: a man whose cruelty is matched only by his frightening intelligence. I'm sure you know whom I'm referring to by now. But let me first solve the mystery of the locked room and provide concrete evidence for my suspicions. Please—follow me next door.'

Mr Ishikari stopped me. 'Koichi, there's one thing I don't understand. Why would this horrific murder method be hinted at in a poem Hisako wrote in her diary five years ago? Did Hisako know how her father had been murdered? Or was she already predicting the murders that would take place five years later?'

'I thought long and hard about this myself. The exact sequence of events seemed impossible to determine. However, eventually, I arrived at a horrifying yet logical explanation.

'It was just before the first of the recent murders. After telephoning Akimitsu at his hotel, when I came upstairs and made to knock on Taijiro's door, I was shocked to overhear a quite unsettling conversation. First I heard these chilling words, spoken by Rintaro:

'*You really want to take her out? After everything? All our efforts will have been for nothing. Well, as you please. It's all rather ridiculous, anyway.*

'Then came Taijiro's even more unnerving reply:

'*I'm telling you, something bad is going to happen. I don't know what, exactly, but I can feel it. I really do think, for my own safety as much as anything, that getting rid of her is the only way to proceed.*

'I stood there, hesitating to knock on the door. In the end I decided to come and wait in this room instead.

'Clearly, Taijiro and Rintaro were planning some kind of murder. I hardly think they would have spoken that way if it were only some canary or mad dog they wanted to put down. In which case, who was the intended victim? Obviously it can't have been Taijiro, although in the event he was killed later that very evening.

'If they were able to discuss the murder so casually, it was because this was a killing that would take place completely out of sight. Taijiro was worried their crime of ten years ago was going to come to light. Now, who else knew about that secret? They didn't need to worry about Hisako; she had already lost her mind. Kenkichi was a child and wouldn't remember the events of a decade ago. No, there was only one person Taijiro was worried about, and one person he feared. That person was Kayoko Chizui.

'Now, you might be wondering what all this has to do with your question, but remember: Hisako lost her virginity to this demonically cruel man; that is a fact. Let us imagine that at some point he also revealed the savage murders he was plotting to her; in that case, what could she do to try and stop them? Rintaro and the others held her mother's life in their hands. If she went to the police, they'd ensure Kayoko was killed before she could be rescued, and there'd be no one left to testify to their crime. There was no one Hisako could turn to. That must have been what impelled her to write that poem. Unable to record the truth openly, she smuggled it into those verses instead. It wasn't long afterwards that she lost her mind completely. Fortunately, the poem survived, intact and unnoticed—and now, five years later, the heinous crimes it foretold have finally come to pass …'

10

The Demon in the Locked Room

(Koichi Yanagi's journal, continued)

For a moment, Mr Ishikari, Yoshino, Kenkichi and I remained silent, each sunk deep in our own thoughts. The meaning concealed in the lines of the poem had been more awful than anyone could have guessed.

Just then, there was a quiet knock at the door.

'Master Kenkichi?' called the maid. 'Rintaro says he'd like to see you.'

What could he be plotting this time? Was he trying to taunt me somehow?

Kenkichi looked up at me. He was trembling from head to toe.

'Go on, you'll be okay,' I said, patting him on the shoulder encouragingly. The expression of alarm on his face was understandable. His eyes, too, seemed to fill with some deep, ineffable meaning. Wordlessly, he made his way downstairs with the maid. There was no time to waste, I realized. Tomorrow would be too late. I decided I would have to make the first move; it was time to rip Rintaro's challenge to shreds.

I gestured to Yoshino and Mr Ishikari to follow me. 'Gentlemen, time is running short. Let me show you how the locked-room murder was carried out. Inspector Yoshino, we'll need an additional pair of hands—could you get someone? One of your officers will suffice.'

Yoshino opened the window and called to the young police-man stationed outside, who hurried upstairs and stood to attention in front of us.

'Well then, let's begin.'

By this point, they all seemed quite in awe of my deductive skills. We made our way into Taijiro's room, where the first murder had taken place. The door frame still bore the signs of our break-in, only adding to the bleak atmosphere that prevailed inside.

'Inspector Yoshino, yesterday I asked the police to return the Noh mask. Were you able to bring it with you today?'

Yoshino produced a cloth bundle and unwrapped it to reveal the terrible mask. It had been two days since I had last set eyes on that demonic face. Even in the broad summer daylight, it sent a fresh chill through my heart.

I murmured some instructions into the ear of the young policeman. He nodded, then walked off to make his way up to the attic.

'Gentlemen, I will now reveal the method by which this room was sealed after Taijiro's murder. We know how the murder itself was carried out; the mystery concerns the mechanical trick by which the door and windows were sealed. I was one of the last people to visit Taijiro while he was alive. In fact, I was probably the last person to enter or leave the room before the murderer himself. Only two elements of this room changed after my departure: the pivot windows and the mask. As far as I recall, when I left the room, the pivot windows were still open. And, of course, the mask was not lying on the floor.

'Two nights before the first murder, a masked figure appeared in the window, giving Mr Ishikari and myself a fright. But by the time we rushed into the room, joined by Taijiro, the only person we found was Hisako.

'Taijiro was all too aware of the shameful crime he'd colluded in ten years ago, and so the appearance of that masked figure must have come as quite a shock. He realized that behind that bizarre sight lurked a most sinister intention. That was when he decided to nip the problem in the bud by killing Kayoko; he also asked me to enlist Akimitsu as his detective. But the murderer was smarter than Taijiro. After overhearing his phone call to the hotel and realizing the urgency of the situation, he used the method I outlined a moment ago in order to kill his own father—using the Noh mask to suggest that the heart attack had merely been triggered by a psychological shock.

'This morning, Akimitsu told me Sawako had to be the murderer. He even suggested a method by which she had supposedly sealed the room. It involved passing a metal skewer through the hole in the shank of the key, then tying a piece of string to the tip of the skewer. The other end of the string would then be attached to a weight that was let out of one of the pivot windows. The string could then be pulled from below, turning the key in the lock. Tugging on it further would pull the skewer out of the pivot window and down onto the ground.

'Now, that's certainly an interesting theory, but the question is: how would you close the pivot window afterwards? From inside, you can simply pull on a cord to close it. From outside all it would take is a gentle push—but the problem is the location: at the top of a first-floor room, at least six metres above the ground, with no handholds or footholds on the wall. In other words, closing one of those pivot windows from ground level would be exceedingly difficult—especially if you were trying to avoid being seen.

'But there's one thing that's been overlooked. What if the door was locked not from the ground below, but from the attic

172

above? In fact, it would be almost impossible to successfully—and discreetly—seal that room from anywhere else.

'I will now conduct an experiment to show you precisely what I mean. But before that, we must establish the role played by the Noh mask. Notice how a lump of lead has been attached to one of its horns. Why might that have been done? Certainly, it adds a bit of weight, but it's not like the murderer used the mask to bludgeon his victim to death …

'Allow me a brief diversion. You may have heard about the recent spike in foreign demand for traditional long-nosed *tengu* masks. Buoyed by this wave of enthusiasm, mask makers started mass-producing other stock characters, such as the plump-faced Okami and the gurning Hyottoko—but it seems they've barely sold a single one. You see, it appears the sudden interest in *tengu* masks had nothing to do with their function as actual masks; instead, they were merely being prized for their long noses, which made for an eccentric hat peg in Western homes.

'Now, all this may seem rather trivial. But I assure you that it points us in the direction of a more disturbing truth. If the distinctive feature of a *tengu* is its long nose, then what is it that sets the *hannya* apart?

'I'm sure you've guessed the answer. The mask is, of course, distinguished by the length of its horns. The other day, Akimitsu informed me that the mask before us now is technically not a *hannya* but a *jya* mask—in other words, one with even longer horns. Such pedantry is of no interest to us; all I want you to focus on are these two sharp and slightly curved horns. Why? Because they were used to turn the key. A bizarre idea, I know. But it was precisely the mask's presence at the scene of this murder-by-heart-attack that convinced everyone that this was a locked-room murder of the "psychological shock" type.

'Recall those bottles of sulphuric acid and zinc that were missing from the laboratory, and which we discovered in the darkroom upstairs. Those two substances played a crucial role in sealing the room. By combining them, the murderer was easily able to produce hydrogen.

'Gentlemen, have you ever watched one of those balloon sellers at a fair? They put some zinc or scrap iron into a bottle, then pour in sulphuric acid. Then they seal the bottle with a bung, pass a narrow bamboo tube through the bung and use the resulting contraption to inflate their balloons. With that in mind, the other prop used by the murderer should come as no surprise.'

I reached into my box and produced the rubber balloon I had filled with hydrogen in the laboratory. I attached a long piece of twine to it, then let it out of one of the pivot windows. We peered out to watch as the balloon floated upwards, passed by the attic window and stopped when it was approximately level with the roof.

'Inspector Yoshino, could you hold this for me?' I said, handing him the twine. 'Careful you don't let go.'

I picked up the mask, made my way over to the door and inserted the key into the lock. To seal the door, it needed to turn clockwise. Holding the mask so that it was upside down and facing me, I lowered its right horn through the hole in the key's shank. Then I took the twine back from Yoshino, tied a loop in the end of it, passed the thread through a ring built high into the wall by the door and placed the loop around the mask's left horn.

'Right, everything's ready. You'll have noticed that I was able to set up the entire mechanism on my own. Once the murderer had made these preparations, he carefully opened the door, went out into the hall and closed the door without dislodging the mask. Then he made his way up to the attic and pulled on the thread of the balloon outside the window. For the sake of brevity, let's speed things up a little.' I opened the window and called to the policeman in the attic. 'Could you pull on that thread, please?'

We watched as the thread began to move. The Noh mask, which had kept its balance because of the lead attached to its right horn, now glared at us from its upside-down position on the door. Inch by inch, the thread crawled in the direction of the window. As the left horn slowly rose, the key began to rotate clockwise in the lock. Soon the mask was on its side, and before long it had turned a full one hundred and eighty degrees. At this point, the right horn slipped out of the key shank and the mask clattered onto the floor. Simultaneously, the loop came free from the left horn. The thread whipped through the ring in the wall, out of the pivot window and off into the sky.

Next, the officer in the attic lowered a short pole and gave the pivot window a firm push. The window swung shut, and the spring-loaded latch clicked into place. The room had been completely sealed. I turned to Mr Ishikari and Inspector Yoshino, my expression calm.

'Well, gentlemen, *that* is how you seal a room using a Noh mask. Of course, the pivot windows run the length of the room, so it's impossible to say which one the murderer used. In any case, their height above the floor turned out to be an advantage. Rather than letting the thread fall down to the ground, the murderer realized he could use a balloon to make it go upwards and then pull on it from the attic window. It was quite the ingenious idea—and one which had us all completely baffled. I was only alerted to the possibility when we discovered the sulphuric acid and zinc in the darkroom.

'Disposing of the thread was easy: all the murderer had to do was let go and the balloon would float off into the sky. Even if it were eventually discovered somewhere, nobody would ever suspect the horrific purpose it had served.

'In other words, this was a locked-room murder of the mechanical variety. Still, it exhibited some rather unusual features. Particularly striking was the fact that the cause of death was a heart attack, which helped to imply the murder had been achieved by some kind of psychological shock. Indeed, when you factor in the use of the Noh mask as a prop, it's hardly surprising that this was initially assumed to be a "psychological" variant of the locked-room murder.

'But there was one fatal flaw in the murderer's plan. Given the direction in which the thread needed to travel, there was, in fact, only one location from which it could have been pulled: the darkroom in the attic. It was as though the murderer was pointing a finger at himself.

'Still, he seems to have had a pretty low opinion of our detective skills. Arrogantly assuming that mere mortals like us were no match for the superhuman genius of his stratagem, he didn't even bother to remove the zinc and sulphuric acid from the darkroom. And if you follow me up there now, I'll show you my last piece of evidence.'

By this point I was sure I'd won them over completely. I led the way up to the attic.

The policeman who'd helped pull the thread was waiting in the darkroom. Brushing him aside, I showed Mr Ishikari and Inspector Yoshino the photograph of Hisako on the wall. Like me, they visibly flinched at the sight.

Sometimes, even those who are used to dealing with violent crimes can experience a strange terror when they hear about some seemingly trivial act that was carried out afterwards. I'd once heard about a murder case—a spur-of-the-moment kill-ing, born from a fit of rage. The head of a restaurant kitchen had scolded one of his chefs for something petty, and the chef had suddenly flown off the handle and stabbed him to death with a carving knife. The chef had immediately turned him-self in to the police, and ended up getting off with a five-year sentence. I didn't find any of this particularly unsettling in itself. But when I learned that, immediately after the murder, the chef had carefully washed his knife under the tap, placed it back on the rack where it belonged, and only then gone to turn himself in—it sent a shiver down my spine. Perhaps he washed his knife purely out of habit. But to have carried out such a mundane, mechanical action, as if he had simply finished preparing a cut of fish or beef, in the aftermath of a horrific murder—I could only shudder at the strangeness of the human mind.

There is something in all of us that pulls us back from the brink of complete brutality. Even the most depraved criminal carries something deep inside that will prevent him from, say, desecrating the corpse of his victim. If someone does cross that line, all we can do is turn away in revulsion. Rintaro's actions were precisely such an aberration. He had taken his cousin's virginity; he had triggered her complete derangement; and yet that still hadn't been enough for him …

I showed Mr Ishikari and Inspector Yoshino the bottles of sulphuric acid and zinc. They could only nod in silence.

'Now, I'm sure you've noticed the jasmine-like fragrance filling this room. You see, in the end, it was the murderer's own body that let him down. He knew he needed to conceal the smell of ether, and decided to use an even more potent jasmine perfume to do so. But that meant using the fragrance on three separate occasions. Each time, he brought a little bit of it back with him to this darkroom, where it still lingers. The problem, of course, was that he didn't notice …

'You both know whom I am talking about. The man who conspired in the killing of Soichiro Chizui ten years ago, and was therefore well versed in the horrifying method of murder used in all these crimes; the man who robbed Hisako of her virginity, and confided such diabolic crimes to her that she could only conceal them in a poem before eventually losing her mind; the man who had the perfectly sane Kayoko committed to a mental asylum for ten years, ultimately resulting in her death; the man who was here in the attic on the night of the first murder—and who, having lost his sense of smell, failed to notice the fragrance that still pervades this room. That man, gentlemen, is none other than Rintaro Chizui.'

A deathly hush settled in the darkroom. Mr Ishikari and Inspector Yoshino were visibly shaken, though a grim determination also lined their faces.

Victory was finally mine. Now even the demoniacal Rintaro would have no choice but to capitulate. I opened the window and looked down at the rolling waters of Tokyo Bay. The bracing sea breeze that swept into the room felt pleasant on my flushed cheeks. I stared up into the wide open sky. In the corner of my vision, a seabird tucked its wings and plummeted towards the sea.

But this moment of calm did not last long. Yoshino was the first to break the silence.

'Thank you, Mr Yanagi. I think we can now consider the Chizui murders a closed case. Prosecutor, we mustn't repeat the mistake we made with Sawako. I'd like to arrest Rintaro Chizui at once.'

'Wait a moment, Inspector—let's not rush things. Now, Koichi's theory is quite remarkable. He has solved the mystery that lurked within the Chizui family all these years. We might have been too late to save Kayoko, but we can assume she was sane all along; and we also found that radium. His sharp deduction has revealed the truth about everything—from the chilling method behind the murders, to the way in which the room was sealed, to the real purpose of that Noh mask. But unfortunately, that's all it is—deduction. There isn't a shred of direct evidence. I fully understand your desire to arrest Rintaro. But without hard proof, I'm not convinced we'll have much of a case against him …'

Mr Ishikari slowly raised a hand to his brow as he pursued his thoughts. He didn't even seem to notice the ash tumbling from his cigarette onto the floor.

'You know what? I think it's time to spring a little psychological trap on him. In the hall just now, he told me he'd reveal the murderer's name at one o'clock this afternoon. Have you heard, Koichi? He wants to bring tomorrow's showdown forward to today. Sawako's suicide must have him spooked. He's gunning for a face-off, Koichi; I hope you're ready for whatever he's got planned.'

I didn't mind in the least. Indeed, I felt confident I was one step ahead. A confrontation with the monstrous Rintaro—wasn't that precisely what I'd been expecting when I first decided to solve these murders? He might have been the one to throw down the gauntlet, but I was spoiling for the fight.

'Oh, don't you worry. I think I know what he's plotting: he wants to claim I'm the murderer. He'll use that clever brain of his to contrive all sorts of evidence against me. But rest assured: I'll demolish whatever theory he comes up with. What's more, I reckon we'll be able to get our hands on that direct evidence you mentioned.'

I couldn't back down, not now. Mr Ishikari seemed to understand exactly where I was coming from: for the first time in a while, a smile had spread across his features.

'Let's go back downstairs,' he said. 'I can't bear to stay in here a moment longer.'

We made our way downstairs and into the spare room with the piano. Mr Ishikari sank onto one of the sofas, lit a cigarette, then turned to me.

'Koichi, in both Noh and Kabuki, the demon always appears wielding a prop of some kind. What do you suppose it was this time?'

I still didn't see what he was getting at. Hadn't I already established the role of the Noh mask in the case? And yet Mr Ishikari seemed fixated on these theatrical distractions.

'Well, I suppose it would have to be the spray of maple leaves and the snake-scale costume, wouldn't it?'

'No, those were just window dressing,' he murmured, half to himself. 'I'm talking about the first murder. What was the prop, Koichi?'

He appeared to sink deep into thought. We heard the quiet yet piercing chime of the clock on the mantelpiece. It was eleven o'clock: just two hours until the face-off.

'Inspector Yoshino? Phone for you.'

Yoshino nodded in response to the officer who had delivered this message and disappeared downstairs. It was just Mr Ishikari and me now. The air seemed laced with dread. Was this the calm before the storm?

I decided to vent a thought that had been on my mind for some time.

'Mr Ishikari, the law can be quite a vexing thing. Can we really do nothing in the face of a monster like Rintaro? All you prosecutors seem to care about is direct evidence and confessions of guilt. Ultimately, you're little more than slaves to the law, aren't you?'

'Koichi, if you don't mind, that's an odd way of looking at things. If there's one thing we care about above all else, it's maintaining the social order. Where we have a solid case against someone, backed by hard evidence, we take firm action. And in the face of the most terrible crimes, we'll seek the death penalty. But then my conscience will be clean; I will only have carried out my prescribed duty in the name of justice and humanity.'

Mr Ishikari spoke quietly. Perhaps unsurprisingly, given his long years of service as a public prosecutor, his words carried a rock-solid certainty.

'But is the law really capable of punishing a criminal like Rintaro?' I asked. 'Even supposing he's arrested for these murders, imagine what would have happened if he hadn't committed them. The law would have completely failed to punish the actions of a man so diabolical that he helped kill his own uncle, imprisoned his aunt in a mental asylum and robbed his cousin of both her virginity and her sanity. He planned a murder and had someone else carry it out; he deprived his own aunt of her freedom and had her subjected to unwarranted abuse; he trampled all over a young woman's life simply because he felt like it. And your laws did nothing. Mr Ishikari, if society fails to protect the weak and honourable, then self-styled "supermen" like Rintaro will go on exploiting the law in order to sate their own desires, and we'll never be rid of their despicable presence on this earth.'

'Koichi, I'll be the first to admit that the law isn't perfect. Rintaro is a truly execrable man, and yet you're right: if it wasn't for these murders, he'd probably have remained out of the law's grasp forever. But—and I say this not as a prosecutor but simply as your fellow man—I believe that even those who evade the law can never escape the judgement of heaven. The murders of the last few days are a case in point. Three individuals who evaded society's laws have, in the end, received the harshest of divine punishments.'

'Interesting. Are you suggesting the gods have simply used a human to carry out their will on earth? That Rintaro's deranged fantasies caused him to murder his own family one by one—and in the process dig his own grave? That would certainly be quite the ironic fate ...'

'Koichi, there is a great, invisible force at work in our society. You might compare it to the action of white blood cells in our body. To protect us from foreign substances, our body secretes antibodies that counteract them and minimize the damage done. Society sustains its own health in much the same way. So it is that in societies with only primitive legal systems, revenge is an accepted form of justice. If it helps prevent murders rooted in pure wickedness, and stops that wickedness from spreading through society, it may be viewed as a necessary evil.'

'So are you endorsing the idea of revenge?'

'Not at all. Under our modern legal system, revenge as a form of justice is unconscionable. I'm simply acknowledging its role in the evolution of that system.'

'Then do you think that in the future, when the law has evolved even further, it will finally be capable of punishing a criminal like Rintaro?'

'Oh, yes. Just look at the war crimes tribunal happening in Tokyo. Previously, there was no basis in international law for trying someone for their individual responsibility in a war. Now that idea has come into question. So you see, the law is constantly evolving.'

'I suppose even in feudal Japan, when the concept of revenge itself was admired, there were still cases where it had to be punished for the sake of the social order ...'

'Precisely, Koichi. Just look at what happened when the Forty-Seven Ronin avenged the death of their master. Popular as their actions were, that moral stance was a relic of the feudal era; indeed, some would argue it was a futile and foolish undertaking. And so even under the law of that time, the punishment that was handed down was that they were "granted death", as the phrase went—in other words, allowed to take their own lives.

'But even our most futile-seeming actions can serve a purpose. Why is it that certain deeds, though our rational brain might deem them wrong, are nonetheless so capable of appealing to our emotions? Acts of pure altruism, transcending self-interest; a yearning for justice; the urge to stop evil in its tracks: when all is said and done, aren't those the things that move us most?'

'Indeed,' I said, 'when we read stories as children, we were always immediately able to recognize the characters as either good or bad. There was no in-between; that wasn't allowed. We might be older now, but I feel as though part of us will always want the world to be that way.'

'Yes, I think you're right ...' Mr Ishikari broke off as Yoshino burst into the room.

'Sir, I've just had some good news on the phone. It's been confirmed that Kayoko Chizui was sane all along. Doctor Oka and his team of nurses denied everything at first, but we obtained testimony from some of the other doctors and nurses who didn't look too kindly on what they were doing. Witness after witness spoke out, until in the end Doctor Oka was forced to confess everything. It turns out he accepted a huge sum of money from Taijiro Chizui to keep Kayoko in confinement ...'

'Was Rintaro involved?'

'Doctor Oka said he wasn't sure. He's met Rintaro several times, but apparently the topic never came up. But this is still enough, isn't it? I mean, it seems completely implausible that he'd have no idea what his own father was up to, given that they lived in the same house ...'

Mr Ishikari's face had taken on a look of fresh grief. With his hands clasped behind his back and his head tilted straight downwards, he paced around the room in silence.

'Thank you, Yoshino,' he said eventually, in a low and slightly trembling voice. 'I've made my decision. Whatever it takes, we simply cannot allow Rintaro Chizui to remain free. He is an enemy of humanity; a defiler of the law. Still, let's give him one more hour. No doubt he still thinks beating us will be a cinch. I want to see exactly how he digs his own grave.'

The cool gaze of the prosecutor had disappeared from Mr Ishikari's eyes; instead they burned with fierce resolve.

He turned to me. 'Akimitsu said he gave you a piece of paper he found on the stairs—a shorthand transcript of Taijiro's phone call to the hotel. Do you have it now?'

'Yes, it's in this folder.'

'Could you show me it?'

I opened up the folder I'd been carrying around. But to my surprise, the transcript was missing.

'I'm sure it was in here ...' I said, looking up at him.

'Strange. And you haven't let it out of your sight?'

Mr Ishikari's tone was serious.

'Just twice—when I joined you for Sawako's questioning, and when we went to find the radium in the laboratory. I left it on the desk in the study.'

'So it was unattended,' he replied, the tension growing in his voice. 'Come on, you two—we'll do a quick search.'

The study seemed unchanged from before. Mr Ishikari scanned the room, wordlessly taking in its every detail. But nothing seemed out of the ordinary.

Eventually, he crouched down and peered into the fireplace.

'Someone has burned a piece of paper here. It's all powder, so there's no way of telling what it was, but I'm sure the ash wasn't here when I came in here just now. It must have been that transcript.'

He stood up and stared pointedly at me.

'Well, Koichi, it looks like you weren't perfect after all. In fact, losing that piece of paper might just be your biggest mistake.'

My mind was reeling. But my hands unconsciously began groping the pockets of my jacket. And there it was: the transcript. I was sure I'd put it in the folder, but in all the excitement I must have slid it into my pocket instead.

'Ah, I'm sorry—I had it here the whole time. Today's been such a blur—I must simply have forgotten where I put it.'

I unfolded the piece of paper on the table and smoothed out the creases. On it was scrawled a series of curved and straight lines.

Mr Ishikari stared at the transcript in apparent disbelief.

'How odd. I was convinced the murderer must have taken it from that folder and disposed of it here. But if you still have it, then what was burnt in the fireplace?'

11

The Final Tragedy

(Koichi Yanagi's journal, continued)

Mr Ishikari ordered Inspector Yoshino to take fingerprints from the transcript, as well as my own for reference. With the showdown with Rintaro looming in less than an hour, I was too agitated to pay much attention.

Then he gave the inspector another order. 'Search the house for another telephone. I have reason to believe another device, in addition to the one in the booth, was used in relation to these murders ...'

With each passing second, the tension in the air was growing more palpable. The maid came to tell us lunch was ready, but I couldn't stomach even the thought of food. Instead, I asked her the question foremost in my mind.

'Where's Rintaro?'

'In the guest bedroom by the dining room. He asked me to bring him his lunch there.'

'Is Kenkichi in there with him?'

'Yes, sir.'

The room in question was on the ground floor, across the hall from the study where we were sitting. Normally it was kept locked and unoccupied, but Rintaro had to have taken Kenkichi in there to grill him about something. In all our interactions, he'd seemed utterly convinced of victory. Did he think that Kenkichi was the ace up his sleeve?

The time quietly passed. At five minutes to one, Yoshino reappeared with an excited look on his face.

'Mr Ishikari, the only fingerprints we found on that transcript were those of Mr Yanagi. But I found another telephone—in the storage closet by the darkroom! The closet was unlocked.'

He showed us the desk telephone he had tucked under his arm. There was barely a speck of dust on it; clearly, it hadn't been in the closet for long.

'Just as I thought,' said Mr Ishikari triumphantly. 'Koichi, what do you make of this?'

'Well, the telephone line exits the house via the attic. If you inserted a needle or something into the wire and connected it up to this telephone, you could listen in to any call made to or from this house.' I felt a thrill of delight; this unexpected new piece of evidence was manna from heaven.

'This blows a hole in Akimitsu's theory, too,' I went on. 'If the hallway wasn't the only place where someone could have eavesdropped on a conversation in the phone booth, then Sawako's story holds up perfectly. In other words, the case against Rintaro is stronger than ever. Not only was the attic the only place from which Taijiro's room could have been sealed, but it was also the easiest location from which to tap the phone wire ...

'I think I've worked out why he wrote that transcript. It was another attempt to flaunt his supposed superhuman ability—to demonstrate that he would always be a step or two ahead of us pathetic mortals. Drunk on that feeling of supremacy, he deliberately left the transcript on the stairs for us to find. Now, if we can just establish that he knows shorthand, then the evidence against him will be insurmountable. Earlier, I had Akimitsu write a note that says "Rintaro is the murderer" in

187

shorthand—the one I gave you just now, Inspector Yoshino. Show it to Rintaro as soon as he gets here, and study his expression. If he shows the slightest reaction, then we have him. We'll rain down blow after blow and wipe that sneer off his face for good.'

Yoshino nodded eagerly.

'Inspector,' said Mr Ishikari, 'post men at the front and back doors—and once we've gone into the dining room, one in the garden outside the room and another in the hall. I hardly expect he'll make a run for it, but we must be prepared for every eventuality.'

Yoshino bowed and left the room. Mr Ishikari turned to me.

'Koichi, could you go up to Hisako's room and fetch the diary where she wrote that poem? I'll be in the dining room.'

I nodded and made my way upstairs. When I entered her room, Hisako sat up in bed and stared blankly in my direction. I instinctively averted my gaze; now was no time to get caught up in my emotions. I grabbed the diary from the desk and hurried back downstairs.

I found Mr Ishikari waiting in the dining room. The main table had been tucked into a corner, and a smaller one, covered with a white tablecloth, placed in the centre of the room with four chairs around it. On the table was the Kutani-ware teacup that Rintaro always drank from, together with three of the cups used for guests. Otherwise, the room was entirely bare.

'Koichi, you sit opposite him. Inspector Yoshino and I will position ourselves between the two of you. Now, don't let your emotions get the better of you. We already have him cornered like a rat—but you know what they say: they're the ones who bite the cat. Don't worry, though—we've made absolutely sure he can't escape.'

I looked him in the eye and nodded. The clock chimed softly; it was one o'clock. Inspector Yoshino walked in.

'Everyone's in position, sir. No sign of him yet?'

'I'm sure he won't be long.'

Mr Ishikari's words were still hanging in the air when the door from the hall slowly opened and the dreaded Rintaro Chizui made his appearance. He seemed as calm and composed as ever, as though he had some kind of plan up his sleeve. He was wearing an immaculate white linen jacket, a well-pressed pair of trousers and an uncreased white shirt, and smiled ironically as he surveyed us. Then he bowed, slowly pulled out a chair, sat down and lit himself a cigarette.

'Mr Chizui, there's something we'd like to show you. We found this in Sawako's room this morning. We can't decipher it, but we wondered if you might be able to?'

Yoshino handed him the note. Rintaro wordlessly took it from him. All our eyes were riveted on his expression.

'Oh, this is Nakane shorthand,' he said coolly. 'It says, "Rintaro is the murderer".'

His tone was decisive, yet casual. His expression hadn't betrayed even a flicker of emotion; even the ash remained on his cigarette. Much as I loathed him, there was a part of me that couldn't help admiring this reckless display of defiance.

'Ah—so you *can* read shorthand, then?' pressed Yoshino.

'Oh, learning it is child's play,' he shot back. 'If you had three days, I'm sure even you could manage to read it, Inspector.'

'I see. Still, Mr Chizui, tell me—is there anyone else who knows shorthand in this household?'

'I believe my deceased sister was able to read it, at least. I don't know of anyone else.'

Yoshino gave us a knowing look. We took our seats.

'Mr Chizui,' began Mr Ishikari sharply, 'we seem to be reaching the final stages of this case. We intend to establish who committed these murders as soon as possible, and then send them to the gallows. So, would you tell us who you believe is behind these crimes?'

'Of course. It's quite simple, really. The murderer is sitting right next to you. The person who planned and executed the Chizui murders is none other than Koichi Yanagi.'

His snake-like eyes flickered unsettlingly in my direction. There was nothing unexpected about his declaration—and yet I could still feel all the blood in my body rushing to my head.

'An interesting claim, certainly,' replied Mr Ishikari without a moment's hesitation. 'But as long as it remains purely in the realm of your imagination, I'm afraid it isn't worth a jot. Would you care to provide evidence?'

'That's a nasty habit you prosecutors have, isn't it? Prattling on about evidence, waggling your magnifying glass about, relentlessly snooping around for your precious clues. You're so obsessed with the worms at your feet that you don't notice the vultures circling overhead. Your law is like a fishing net that only ever catches the small fry; the bigger fish always get away. Go on then, Prosecutor, swing your silly little net!'

He began laughing—a strange, guttural laugh that seemed to come from deep within him. He seemed almost high on his own sarcasm.

'But tell me,' he continued, 'why don't you suspect Koichi here? Apart from the maids, he's the only outsider in the household. And he was spotted close to the scene of all three murders just before they happened. You can't say that of anyone else, can you?'

The smile had vanished from his lips. He was beginning to crank up his attack.

'I suspected him from the start. He was the last one to speak to my father. He sealed the room in order to delay the discovery of the body and give him time to get away from the house. That way, he'd be able to claim he wasn't at home at the time of the murder. I'm sure no one saw my father alive after he left that room ...'

'But ...' said Yoshino, attempting to cut him off. Rintaro merely held up a hand to stop him, then continued his onslaught.

'As for the second murder, it can only have been him or my sister who lured Yojiro out to the gazebo. And we know both of them were near it at the time of his death.

'And on the night of the third murder, Sawako deliberately vacated her bedroom and sneaked off to see Koichi in his cottage. Now, that's hardly admirable behaviour for someone from a respectable family like ours, but I'm sure it was Koichi who seduced her. Truth be told, Sawako didn't have a drop of Chizui blood in her anyway. We had found that out from a blood test. And if our mother had her out of wedlock, I suppose it's hardly surprising that she would attempt something of the sort herself ... Anyway, while she was away from her room, Koichi went into the house. We know that, because the maid saw him.

'You see, Koichi's long spell at the front appears to have taken a huge physical and mental toll on him. That's very unfortunate for him personally, but then fate can be cruel, can't it? When he returned to Japan and found himself without food or shelter, our family welcomed him with open arms. But he failed to see our kindness for what it was.

'Mr Ishikari, I'm sure, as a prosecutor, you are well aware of the recent spike in vicious crimes committed by demobilized soldiers. After all those years on the battlefield, these men have

191

come to see human life as essentially worthless. Day after day, gambling their own lives against those of enemies for whom they felt no personal animosity—it's hardly surprising that killing has become second nature to them. The chilly reception that greeted them when they returned to Japan, coupled with the sense that all their efforts in the war had achieved precisely nothing, filled them with a warped sense of betrayal and resentment.

'And yet they weren't the only ones who paid a terrible price for this long war. Our houses were destroyed; we endured nightmarish air raids and abject living conditions; we only narrowly avoided complete destitution. Somehow, we survived. But the returnees couldn't understand that. Their cold self-interest and emotional indifference were compounded by material poverty and an utter sense of despair. Throwing all ethical considerations to the wind, they have committed crime after heinous crime. Of course, I'm not saying all repatriated soldiers are guilty of such misdeeds. I'm merely talking about the actions of an inevitable minority. Unfortunately, however, Koichi is a member of that minority.

'When he arrived at our house, he pretended to apply himself to the task of producing saccharin and dulcin. In reality, he was slowly preparing his attack. He had become mistakenly convinced that our uncle's death ten years ago was somehow our doing. He realized that if he could somehow bump us off by inducing heart attacks, the suspicion would naturally fall on one of us.

'And it turns out triggering a heart attack is really quite easy. You see, I've had plenty of intravenous shots in my time. Once, a doctor turned to me with a wry smile and said: "You know, Mr Chizui, we doctors could kill plenty of people this way if we wanted. You know how we always squirt the air from the syringe? Well, if we wanted to be rid of someone, all we'd have to do is forget that step and go ahead with the injection. The air would travel down their veins and into their heart. What happens next? A heart attack. There'd be no need for any drugs or special techniques. All we'd need is a syringe—and the patient's trust. It's the perfect murder."

'Of course, the doctor was joking. But after that conversation, I couldn't help feeling a strange shudder whenever a needle was inserted into my arm. Until then, I'd lost all faith in the world's capacity to stimulate or excite me—but from that day on, my world changed. You see, I realized that our innate sense of danger has been slowly numbed by an anaesthetic we call *trust*.

'We are very happy to sit there while a barber shaves our face, without ever suspecting him of any evil intention. Why? Because, inexplicably, we trust him completely. Now I saw that if he harboured the desire to kill me, or perhaps had simply gone insane, there was no telling when he might slip that keen razor of his across my neck. I derived an intense pleasure from this thought. Indeed, I stopped going to my usual barber and began to visit a new—and preferably clumsy-looking—one every time.

'It was the same whenever I rode in a train. I'd close my eyes and imagine the brakes malfunctioning, the driver suffering a moment of madness—or perhaps he'd simply forget to stop, and we'd go careering off the tracks. The passengers would all rise to their feet, shrieking in panic and terror, the windows would shatter … and all the while we'd be gathering speed, racing uncontrollably towards our hellish end.

'And yet, time after time, reality betrayed my imagination. The accidents I so longed for never transpired. When I re-opened my eyes, I'd find the same mediocre scene as ever. The young woman, who, in my fantasy, had wailed for help from a wrecked window, her body mangled by its broken glass, was sitting there knitting in blissful ignorance. The office worker, who was supposed to have been horribly dismembered, was calmly reading his newspaper. By the time I got off the train, I'd be quite disillusioned.

'Before long, I'd reverted back to my usual apathy. So I was quite relieved when a criminal mastermind by the name of Koichi Yanagi appeared in my life. After slaughtering my father, brother and grandmother one by one, he has now turned his attention on me. I can only thank him for it. The sweet horror of not knowing when my own death might come, the thrill of constant suspicion—as sources of excitement go, murder itself pales in comparison.

'When I heard that my father had died of a heart attack, I could only admire Koichi's audacity. If even a layperson like me knew about the injection technique, it was no surprise that a capable scientist like him should too.

'I was convinced I was the third intended victim. Knowing the method he intended to use, I decided I'd seize the opportunity to take him out instead—what kendo fighters call a *go-no-sen*, or simultaneous counter-attack.

'But when the third victim turned out to be my grandmother, I was astonished. It was then that I realized the true extent of Koichi's nefarious scheme. You see, simply murdering me wasn't enough for him. No, he wanted to frame *me* as the murderer—and then watch as I was taken to the gallows.

'Now, I had found the idea that I might be murdered a stimulating one, but the prospect of a worm-like existence on death row—that I simply couldn't stomach. He had finally exceeded the limits of what I considered tolerable. And so I decided to unmask him.

'As for the motive behind his murders—well, I can think of plenty. As I have just explained, I believe the root cause to be the psychological confusion of a returning soldier—combined, no doubt, with a desire to get his hands on our family fortune. With Hisako insane and Kenkichi's health rapidly failing, all he had to do was bump off my father, brother and grandmother, and frame me for their murders, and the entire fortune would fall into the hands of Sawako—who, as he knew very well, was in love with him.

'He may also have been out for revenge, having mistakenly concluded that my family had something to do with my uncle's sudden death ten years ago. In any case, I believe it was some combination of all these motives that drove him to carry out his cold-blooded crimes.'

Rintaro spoke calmly; his face did not betray the slightest emotion. For some time now, he seemed almost to have forgotten I was sitting in front of him—and yet his eyes, with their morbid, reptilian gleam, remained riveted on me.

I couldn't hold back any longer.

'If you want to talk about motives, Rintaro, I'd say you have plenty of your own. I haven't the slightest interest in your family fortune. Just now, I finally worked out that the Professor converted it to a lump of radium worth a colossal sum of money. Now, if I was as greedy as you claim, wouldn't I have kept that discovery to myself? Instead I took these two gentlemen with me to find it, then handed it over to the police for safe keeping. Tell me—are those the actions of a criminal?'

'Radium, eh?' replied Rintaro. 'Interesting. But radium would be quite hard to dispose of by any other means, wouldn't it? A criminal might deliberately entrust it to the police.'

'Still, you admit that one of these so-called motives doesn't hold up. Now, about my relationship with Sawako. Personally,

I'd rather let her rest in peace, but if you're so convinced we were romantically involved, why don't you have her body inspected? If it's a question of whether she was still a virgin, you wouldn't even need to carry out a full autopsy.'

'Oh, I'm well aware of that,' Rintaro shot back.

'Then why don't you go ahead and do it? It would clear things up. This isn't just a question of my innocence—Sawako's reputation hangs in the balance.'

'What, and leave a stain on the Chizui family's honour? No, I refuse to allow it.'

'Honour? Funny, I never expected to hear a word like that in the mouth of a nihilist. You're telling me the man shameless enough to make his deranged cousin pose naked for his camera possesses some miraculous last shred of humanity? Truly, how wonderful! Perhaps we should celebrate the discovery.'

I had given up any attempt at decorum or restraint. There was no longer any point in mincing my words.

'Who said art or beauty has anything to do with good or evil?' he retorted. 'Aesthetic appreciation and morality are quite separate matters.'

'Oh, of course. Beauty without morality, intellect without humanity, power without justice—that's all you've ever cared about, isn't it?'

By now I had completely forgotten the presence of the others in the room.

'Fine,' said Rintaro, 'perhaps your crime wasn't motivated by greed. But what about revenge?'

'Ah, so now you're willingly confessing your old crime. Tell me, what might I be seeking revenge *for*? The murder of Professor Chizui, whose death was so similar to these three killings? The confinement of his perfectly sane wife in a mental asylum? Hisako's disease-induced insanity? Tell me, Rintaro—who, exactly, committed these crimes that you claim I'm avenging?'

'My uncle died from natural causes. And it was my father who arranged Kayoko's hospitalization at the mental asylum, in consultation with Doctor Oka—I wasn't involved at all. Anyway, where's your evidence for this claim that she was sane?'

'Let me help you there,' cut in Yoshino abruptly. 'We investigated the Oka Asylum and gathered statements from various doctors and nurses working there. Doctor Oka eventually cracked under the pressure, confessing that he had, indeed, kept a sane woman in confinement for ten years—all for the sake of a few hundred thousand yen. He claims it was your father who put him up to it, but still, it seems quite implausible to us that you wouldn't have realized what was going on.'

'All I can tell you is that I simply didn't know.'

'Anyway,' I continued, pressing my advantage, 'on the night of the first murder, I went to knock on your father's door and overheard the two of you talking. What were you discussing? Because to me, it sounded awfully like you were planning a murder ...'

'I don't remember that at all,' he replied, as coolly as ever. 'You can't just make things up, Koichi.'

'Gentlemen,' interrupted Mr Ishikari, 'if you both carry on like this, we'll be here all day. Emotional motives and psychological evidence are all well and good, but they won't be enough for us to clear either of you of these murders. Rintaro, you need to provide hard proof that Koichi is the murderer. Koichi has already furnished several pieces of physical evidence indicating that the first murder, at least, could only have been committed by someone in the attic. And on the night of that murder, the only person up there was you, wasn't it?'

'Oh, yes, I was quite alone. There was no one else.'

'And you didn't notice the jasmine-like fragrance in the darkroom?' asked Mr Ishikari, turning up the heat.

'I have severe empyema, you see. I don't pick up on smells unless they're very strong.'

'What about the bottles of sulphuric acid and zinc we found in there?'

'I've no idea what you're talking about.'

'Or the telephone hidden in the closet?'

'This is getting ridiculous. Let's imagine for a minute that these objects had something to do with the murders and I really was the culprit. Wouldn't I want them as far from the crime scene as possible? If anything, the very fact that they were discovered in the darkroom or that closet should point to my innocence. I imagine Koichi hid them there on purpose in order to frame me.'

He simply wouldn't buckle. Indeed, he seemed intent on turning each of our accusations on its head, so that the finger of blame pointed back in my direction every time. But I had one absolute certainty on my side. I had described the only way Taijiro's room could have been sealed. A thread tied to a hydrogen balloon travelled vertically upwards: that was an immutable law of physics. And at the time of the murder, the only person in the room above Taijiro's was Rintaro. I remained confident that I would prevail.

'So, do you have any direct evidence for Koichi being the murderer?'

Rintaro sneered triumphantly at Mr Ishikari's challenge.

'Oh, but of course. Do you really think I'd have accused him otherwise? You see, the problem is his alibi for the first murder. Allow me to demolish it before your eyes. Now, only two people saw my father after Koichi left the house for the Marine Hotel that evening: Sawako and Kenkichi. Sawako claimed she saw my father making a phone call, but who was on the other end of that call? Supposedly, Koichi and Mr Takagi. And if it was Koichi who passed the phone to Mr Takagi, claiming it was my father on the line, Mr Takagi—who had never met him—would be hard pressed to know who he was really speaking to. In other words, it would be very easy for Koichi to dupe him into thinking he was speaking to my father. Someone else made that phone call: Koichi's accomplice. Now, let's come to that person.'

Rintaro spoke breathlessly, his excitement evidently mounting as his monologue gathered pace.

'I don't think we can trust everything Sawako told us. After all, do you remember what she said just before she committed suicide? "There are some secrets a woman can never tell—even if it means carrying them to the grave. I cannot speak of what happened last night, nor shall you ever hear the name of the murderer from these lips." Yes, she knew who was really behind these crimes—and yet she could not speak his name. Why? Because the murderer was also the man she loved. He had killed her father, brother and grandmother, and yet she still couldn't bring herself to reveal his name. There is only one thing that could compel a woman to carry a secret like that to the grave—a profound and passionate love.

'But Sawako also knew perfectly well that her love would never bear fruit. So she decided to end her own life—and take Koichi with her. If her love couldn't be requited in this life, she resolved to make it so in the next. And so she tried to shoot him.

'She also feared that, under further interrogation, she might finally reveal the precious secret. But I can prove that she was lying to you, using logic. It wasn't her father she saw making a

199

phone call that evening, but someone entirely different. And yet for the sake of the man she loved, she was willing to tell a barefaced lie. She did so to save him from the gallows—and yet she ended up paying for that lie with her own life …'

He seemed, by now, entirely oblivious to our presence. He was so enraptured by his own theory that the words simply poured out of him.

Abruptly, as if waking from a dream, he turned to Yoshino.

'Inspector,' he murmured, 'Kenkichi is next door. Bring him in here, would you? Here's the key.'

It was just as I'd guessed. The ace up his sleeve, the accomplice he had concocted for me was none other than Kenkichi Chizui.

A few minutes of tomb-like silence followed. Rintaro's triumphant sneer and Mr Ishikari's worried expression seared themselves, like close-ups in a film, into my retinas.

The door opened again, and Kenkichi appeared, escorted by Inspector Yoshino. His face was so pallid and waxen that for a moment it seemed hard to believe he was even still alive.

'Right then, boy,' said Rintaro, 'tell the prosecutor and the inspector what you told me just now.'

Instinctively we held our breath.

There was a pause. Then Kenkichi cried out: 'It was Rintaro! *He* killed my father! *He* put my mother in the asylum! *He* made my sister go mad! Hisako told me everything before losing her mind, but there was nothing I could do … And when Mr Yanagi came to live with us, Rintaro took advantage of his presence to kill Uncle Taijiro, Yojiro and Grandmother, who knew about his crimes, then tried to frame Mr Yanagi for their murders! He cornered me just now and told me to say I'd lied about my uncle coming into my room just before he was murdered.

'*Tell them you made that phone call*, he said. He must have eavesdropped on the conversation somehow—he knew everything they'd talked about. He told me if I didn't do as he said, he'd take my life—as well as my sister's. I was so scared I said I'd obey. But the truth is … the truth is … *he's the murderer!*'

Kenkichi levelled a trembling finger at Rintaro's chest. He was biting his lips so hard they were bleeding; his breath was ragged, his small chest heaving with every inhalation.

Rintaro got to his feet. For the first time, he appeared quite unsettled.

'You little bastard …'

If not for our presence, he might have pounced on Kenkichi and throttled him to death there and then. But even as we watched, something was happening to the boy. Dark red blood trickled from the edge of his mouth, down his pale chin and onto his white shirt. Then he collapsed to the floor, his small body crumpling in the doorway. His finger still pointed at Rintaro.

Mr Ishikari rushed over and cradled Kenkichi in his arms. 'Poison …'

As he uttered the word, he shot Yoshino a decisive look. The inspector immediately sprang into action.

'Rintaro Chizui, I am arresting you for the Chizui family murders.'

Rintaro slumped into his chair, folded his arms and, for a brief moment, closed his eyes. Then, as if desperately trying to rethink his strategy in the face of certain defeat, he reached for his cup of tea for the first time and gulped the entire thing down.

He did not respond to Yoshino's orders to stand up. Instead, his knees and hands began to convulse. His breath became laboured and rasping. His eyes closed again – this time for good. He clutched desperately at the tablecloth in front of him, slowly pulling it to one side. Then, before our eyes, his face growing paler by the second, Rintaro tumbled out of his chair and onto the floor, dragging the cloth with him.

The three of us stood there dumbfounded, staring at the body on the floor. In the end, Rintaro really had dug his own grave.

Yoshino picked up a small paper package lying by Rintaro's feet and gave it a quick sniff before handing it to Mr Ishikari.

'Cyanide …' they murmured in unison.

'Well,' said Mr Ishikari, 'I suppose this brings the Chizui murder case to a close. Inspector, I'm sorry my carelessness has deprived you of his arrest. But the truth is Rintaro would probably have ended up in a mental asylum rather than a prison. Even if we'd arrested him, I'm not convinced we'd have been able to secure a death sentence. His sense of power was all that sustained him. When he realized that his theory had been obliterated, there was nothing left but to take his own life. Deprived of his power, he lost all hope.'

'What about Kenkichi?' asked Yoshino.

'Rintaro was probably worried he'd reveal the truth later on, so he must have slipped him some kind of poison at lunchtime—something that would only take effect an hour or so later. He really was a barbaric man. In all my years as a prosecutor, I've never come across anyone quite so purely evil. It seems that even the most illustrious families can breed men so abominable we can scarcely comprehend them …'

We stood by the two bodies in silence. And when the loud, triumphant laughter of Hisako began to echo from upstairs, mingling with the rumble of distant thunder, it seemed like it would reverberate for ever in our ears, like the finale to the Chizui family murders.

12

The Demise of the Chizui Family

(Hiroyuki Ishikari's letter)

Here ended the journal of Koichi Yanagi. It was three days after the Chizui family murders had reached their brutal conclusion that he presented it to me. I stayed up late that night and read the whole thing. Afterwards, I found myself with some lingering questions, so the following afternoon I left my office early and visited the Chizui mansion. Koichi had told me he would stay at the house until the family's funeral ceremonies were completed.

How many times had I crossed the threshold of that house now? Every time I visited, a new victim seemed to have been sacrificed on the altar of death. The Chizui murder case had ended with Rintaro's suicide. But there remained one final episode in the tragedy.

That day, dark clouds hung low over the mountains and sea. The air, heavy with rain, felt warm against my hands and face; there wasn't even the hint of a breeze. Autumn was just around the corner. Before long, the summer visitors would take their leave of this seaside resort, and it would go back to being a melancholy old fishing village. Approaching the mansion, my step was as heavy as the ponderous clouds overhead.

I stood in the doorway and announced myself to the maid. It wasn't long before Koichi appeared. His face seemed clouded with melancholy.

'Ah, Mr Ishikari. Thank you for coming. Do come in.'

'I hear Hisako isn't doing so well.'

'Indeed. Her condition took an abrupt turn for the worse the night before last. Doctor Yamamoto is rather worried. Says she probably doesn't have long to live ...'

In his eyes I detected an inexpressibly profound grief.

'In that case, I should visit her first.'

We went upstairs and quietly entered Hisako's room. She was fast asleep in her bed. In the space of the past few days, the unmistakeable shadow of death had begun to hang over her features, rendering them almost unrecognizable. Her eyes were sunken and her cheeks hollow, though her long eyelashes remained as beautiful as ever. Her breathing was unsteady, and the stray locks of hair hanging across her brow glistened with sweat.

I took a handkerchief from my pocket and gently dabbed her forehead with it. Despite the thirty years that separated them, I couldn't help but see a shadow of her mother, Kayoko, in her face.

'Koichi, today I've come to see you not as a prosecutor, but as an individual, as your father's dear friend—as Hiroyuki Ishikari. I hope you'll confide in me accordingly.'

He caught my gaze, then nodded. 'Mr Ishikari, I've finally uncovered this family's long-buried secrets; my work here is done. You have been more than a father to me; for that, I thank you from the bottom of my heart. There's nothing I would keep from you.'

'I'm glad to hear that. You know, your journal made quite an impression on me. I just can't shake the feeling that it contains more than it might appear. You haven't lied in the slightest; I believe it to be a very accurate account of events. But there are occasional ... omissions. It is those gaps—and the truth they conceal—that I'd like to ask you about today.

'Before that, though, I'd like you to repeat your demonstration of the locked-room mechanism. I've brought the Noh mask, a rubber balloon and a thread. Do you suppose you could go and fill the balloon with hydrogen in the laboratory?'

For a brief moment, Koichi simply stared at me wordlessly. Then he took the balloon and quietly made his way out of the room.

I stood there, watching Hisako's face as she slept. Before long, warm tears, unseen by anyone, were rolling down my cheeks.

'The balloon's ready, Mr Ishikari. Would you like to get started?'

I followed him into the neighbouring room. Just like last time, he inserted one of the mask's horns into the key and looped one end of the thread around the other. Then he attached the other end of the thread to the balloon and made as if to release it from one of the pivot windows.

'Hang on, Koichi. Could you let it out of the one closest to Hisako's room this time?'

At these words he started on the spot, then turned to look at me. Then, meekly, he did as I'd asked. The balloon pulled the thread out of the window and rose straight up into the sky.

'Well, that's everything ready,' he said, his voice faltering slightly. 'I'll go up to the attic and give the thread a pull. You can stay here and watch.'

'Actually, I think I'll come with you,' I said, and followed him out of the room. After carefully closing the door behind us, he made for the stairs. But I grasped his shoulder.

'Sorry, Koichi. Could we go back into Hisako's room instead?'

He followed me wordlessly. Again, we stood by Hisako's bed. I turned to him.

'Koichi,' I murmured, 'when I mentioned that the demon must have used some kind of prop in the first murder, you

205

seemed quite puzzled. You also overheard me saying to Yoshino and the other officers that if the murder was a Noh performance, it was a "twist on the standard". I learned that much from your journal. Still, you didn't quite understand what I meant, did you? Well, let me explain. You see, the murderer did use a prop—and it really was a twist on the standard.

'In Noh and Kabuki, there's one prop the demon always carries onto the stage—a long cane with a cross bar at the end, known as an *uchizue*. Now, the demon couldn't exactly forget to bring one to this murder, could he? Indeed, the murderer made careful use of his prop. However, it wouldn't be much of a "twist" if he didn't vary the props a little. Look at that ice axe hanging on the wall, Koichi. What does the shape remind you of?'

I quietly gestured towards the ice axe. When he turned back to me, his face was paler than I'd ever seen it.

'Get it down from the wall, then open the window, would you? … Now reach out to the side and use the axe to pull the balloon's thread towards you. Got it? Grab the thread with your hand and give it a tug, would you? Yes, just like that. Once the balloon has come free, use the axe to push and close the window. There we go. Now hang the axe back on the wall, and let's go and see if that door's locked, shall we?'

He was following my instructions like some sort of automaton. I led him into the hallway, then pushed on the door of the neighbouring room. It was locked from inside and wouldn't budge. I turned to Koichi and smiled.

'Quite clever, isn't it? What you referred to in your journal as an "immutable law of physics" turned out to be no match for the demon and his "prop". In other words, Koichi, it turns out there's a flaw in your theory.'

By now he was shaking almost feverishly.

'Your one piece of evidence for Rintaro being the murderer was that the room could only have been sealed by someone in the attic. And it's true that the only person up there was Rintaro. But, as I've just demonstrated, the room could just as easily have been sealed from Hisako's room. So, who really pulled on that thread? How about we go into the spare room and have another look at that journal of yours?'

We made our way into the room with the piano. I opened up the journal and showed it to the disconsolate Koichi.

'Here's what you wrote: *I relieved him of the letter and left the room … After dropping by Hisako and Kenkichi's room for a few minutes, I made my way directly to the Marine Hotel.*

'Well, that's quite the omission! You haven't lied, I suppose. Instead of writing that he handed you the letter, you say you "relieved him" of it—in other words, he wasn't in any state to give it to you. Not only that, but there's no mention of what, exactly, you did during those crucial "few minutes".

'It's the same with the second murder. You write that you led Yojiro to the hall, where you *whispered the instructions into his ear.* But you don't mention what those instructions were, do you? Let's recall the warning Akimitsu gave Yojiro earlier that day: *Whatever anyone says, Koichi and I are the only ones you can trust.* In other words, who else but you, Koichi, could have convinced Yojiro to go out to the gazebo an hour earlier than planned? As for what happened to him there, you write: *I rushed out of the dining room and into the garden, where I checked the gazebo.* But you don't mention what *else* you did there, do you … ? After the deed, it was easy enough to adjust the time on Yojiro's watch to one that gave you an alibi, before dashing it on the rocks.

'Finally, the third murder. You write: *I laid Hisako down on the bed gently and pulled a blanket over her. After another ten minutes or so, I made my way back downstairs.* But what kept you upstairs for those ten minutes? Then: *When I left the laboratory earlier, one of the windows had been unlatched.* I wonder—was that because the latch was broken? Or did you mean, perhaps, that, having a certain purpose in mind, you had deliberately left it open?

'You didn't lie when we questioned you, either. When Inspector Yoshino asked if anything had changed at the scene of the first murder between eight twenty and nine twenty that evening, this is what you told him: *When I left the room, I'm almost certain the pivot windows were still open … Also, the Noh mask wasn't lying on the floor when I left.* Well, quite right. The mask wasn't *on the floor* at that point, it's true. But you didn't tell us where it actually was: suspended upside down, with one of its horns thrust through the shank of the key …

'You have quite a way with words, Koichi: accurate, yet remarkably succinct. I wonder if you picked that up from Agatha Christie's *The Murder of Roger Ackroyd*.

'Still, I can't take the credit for this bit of detective work. No, I wasn't the one who solved this mystery and identified you as the murderer. That was your friend, Akimitsu Takagi.

'You see, in writing your journal, you made one fatal mistake. When Yojiro came to see you two at the hotel, you report that Mr Takagi *had written in shorthand*: YOJIRO CHIZUI IS THE MURDERER. And yet there's no indication, before or afterwards, that he read out to you what he'd written. In other words, this was a clear admission that you know shorthand. Quite the slip-up, I must say.

'Rintaro was right to accuse you of using Kenkichi as an accomplice. Desperate to establish yourself an alibi, you asked him to make that phone call to the hotel. It can't have been too hard to pull off—after all, once a boy's voice has broken, it's surprisingly hard to distinguish it from an adult's. Mr Takagi was hardly likely to notice anything strange about the voice of someone he'd never met—much less when he was speaking to him over the telephone. Still, you didn't have time to discuss with Kenkichi exactly what he should say. Instead, you scribbled out his lines in shorthand on a piece of paper and gave it to him to read over the phone. In other words, the shorthand note wasn't a record of that phone conversation—it was the script for it.

'But when Kenkichi somehow managed to drop the note on the stairs, it became a crucial piece of evidence against you. I suppose, being only fourteen, he didn't quite realize the seriousness of what he was mixed up in. When you saw that the note had found its way into Mr Takagi's hands, you must have been aghast. But the fact that he had not yet handed it in to the police offered you a glimmer of hope. Knowing his personality all too well, you deliberately told him to submit it as evidence, and in doing so managed to persuade him to do the opposite. When that plan worked, you must have breathed a sigh of relief. But Mr Takagi was even more meticulous than you realized. Without telling any of us, he asked an acquaintance of his in the police to check the note for fingerprints. That was precisely what you'd feared. You'd worn gloves when you committed your murders—but not when you wrote out your note.

'When Mr Takagi was informed that the fingerprints on the note matched the ones on your whisky glass at the hotel, he was flabbergasted. What was even harder to fathom was the presence of Kenkichi's prints on the paper.

'In your journal, Mr Takagi comes across as a complete idiot, but it seems a correction is called for. Nobody is perfect, after all. Making mistakes is only human. Solving a crime is never a smooth or methodical process—unless, of course, the criminal were to record their every action in a journal …

'But it seems Mr Takagi was deeply moved by the way you acted at the Oka Asylum. Having vaguely surmised the motive behind your murders, he began to empathize with your decision to commit them. He couldn't bring himself to hand his dear friend over to the police. Instead, he took me to one side and explained the situation, then left your fate in my hands. He told me he'd forget everything he'd learned, then withdrew entirely from the case. Be grateful to that man, Koichi. See how, even in a situation like this, friendship shows us its beautiful light.

'Before leaving the mansion for good, he handed you a duplicate version of the supposed "transcript" and asked me to observe your reaction. But you didn't notice the switch. Shorthand is more like a series of pictures than handwriting in the conventional sense. It's very hard even for experts to analyse forensically—which means, conversely, that it's very easy to forge.

'Still, you did suspect that Mr Takagi might have told me or the police about the note. Therefore, worrying that someone might find Kenkichi's fingerprints on it, you decided to burn it and create a new one—without, of course, realizing that what you'd created was a copy of a copy. Let's return to your journal. Here's what you wrote: *I went into the neighbouring study, retrieved the folder containing the shorthand transcript Akimitsu had given me, made a few final preparations, then left the room.* Once again, none of this is untrue. But you've cunningly avoided explaining what these "final preparations" of yours actually involved—disposing of the evidence in the fireplace.

'But in fact you had committed another fatal error. In trying to get rid of something you thought could hurt you, you ended up destroying something you desperately needed. You couldn't have anyone finding Kenkichi's fingerprints; as for your own, it was only natural for them to be on the paper, since Mr

Takagi had handed it to you. But what about Mr Takagi's own fingerprints—why on earth would *they* be missing from the piece of paper? This was the fundamental problem with your forged version of the note.

'You may have destroyed Mr Takagi's duplicate. But a comparison of the original note, which Mr Takagi entrusted to me, and the third version, which *you* gave me, is still enough evidence, my dear Koichi, for me to indict you as the person behind the Chizui family murders.'

At some point, Koichi's eyes had grown moist with tears. I rose from my chair and stood by the window, where I watched, in weary silence, the rolling white crests of the waves below.

Presently I returned to my seat.

'Koichi, I hope you realize that my actions stem from the profound regard I have for you. I came to see you today not as a prosecutor, but as your friend, Hiroyuki Ishikari. I've never let my personal feelings interfere with the application of the law—but just this once, I find myself forced to break with that precedent.

'Something about your motive in committing these crimes touched me deeply. Try as you might to conceal your emotions in the journal, I could feel your hatred of Rintaro and your love for Hisako on its every page. So, why don't you tell me everything? You were out for revenge, weren't you?'

'You're quite right, Mr Ishikari,' said Koichi. There was a strange, beautiful glint in his tearful eyes. 'I wanted revenge for a buried crime—one the law had failed to punish.'

'They may have avoided sentencing in a court, but in the end there was no escaping the judgement of heaven. Before you knew it, you'd become an agent of divine justice ... Now, my first question is about that poem in Hisako's diary. Who wrote it? It was you, wasn't it?'

'That's right. I arranged for a friend to send it on to Hisako. You see, it was during the war that I realized the horrifying truth behind Professor Chizui's death. I also began to guess at the circumstances behind his wife's confinement in a mental asylum. I could hardly bring myself to imagine what had happened; it seemed almost too horrific to be true. In my dreams, over and over again, I pictured how I would get my revenge. An eye for an eye, and a tooth for a tooth—that was all I wanted. And so I wrote a poem that secretly hinted at my planned revenge and sent it to Hisako.'

'But the poem also hinted at something else: your relationship with Hisako. The two of you were deeply in love. Tell me, did you know her painful secret?'

'I did. If Rintaro managed to trick her into sleeping with him that once, it was only because she didn't know the first thing about sex. Of course, neither of us realized the terrible consequences it would have for her later.'

'I see. It's all just as I thought. So when you arrived at the Chizui mansion and saw just how deranged Hisako had become, I suppose you could no longer control your rage—or your appetite for revenge.'

'Exactly. My hatred for the Chizui family had exceeded the limits of what I could bear. Revenge for the Professor; revenge for Kayoko; revenge for Hisako. I planned to kill three of the culprits using the same method they had used on the Professor, frame Rintaro for the murders and free Kayoko from her imprisonment. Rintaro had colluded in a murder, confined a perfectly sane woman in a mental asylum for ten years and deprived an innocent young woman of her virginity and her sanity—all without getting his own hands dirty. I thought it would only be fitting, therefore, if he were executed for crimes he did *not* commit.'

'Indeed. Part of me agrees with your decision, Koichi; your horrific paradox makes a certain kind of sense. One woman with a clear psychological impairment remains at home, while another, entirely sane, is confined in a mental asylum for a whole decade. A monster who evaded the clutches of the law for the crimes he *did* commit is framed for ones he had nothing to do with and ends up taking his own life as a consequence.

'The Chizui mansion was not a place where normal notions of justice held much sway. In that house where nothing made sense and only wickedness seemed to prevail, you decided to fight fire with fire.

'I must say, your use of the locked room was quite ingenious. Not only did you prevent the body from being found until after you'd had time to leave the house and then return, thereby creating a rock-solid alibi, but your use of the balloon made it seem as though the murderer must have been operating from the attic. But tell me—why did you decide to involve Mr Takagi in the case?'

'It was vital that I only step into my role of detective later on; at first, I wanted to act merely as a sort of sidekick. The idea was to use Akimitsu as a sort of robot for my ends.'

'But he wasn't quite the idiot you'd imagined and ended up being more like the monster to your Frankenstein. True, he eventually stepped back and allowed you to take over. But by that point he already knew your terrible secret.

'Do you know what he told me just before he left? It was just after I'd mentioned that I'd asked you to record these events in a journal. He smiled sadly at me and said: "Perhaps it's wrong for me to compare Koichi's personal struggle to a detective novel. But knowing him the way I do, and given the events of ten years ago and everything he discovered at the Oka Asylum, I think that journal of his might end up forming

213

the basis for a detective novel with an entirely unprecedented format." As he explained, it's not that rare for the detective or indeed the narrator to turn out to have been the murderer—but a novel where the narrator, detective and murderer are all the same person would be something entirely new. Now, Mr Takagi seemed to want me to think he was merely joking, but the tears I glimpsed in his eyes suggested otherwise … In any case, your attempt to use him as a mere puppet was, perhaps, your greatest mistake.

'You even provided us with a detailed explanation of how the murder was carried out. You simply never told us that the murderer was you … The bottles of zinc and sulphuric acid in the darkroom, the jasmine perfume sprinkled on the bodies—that was all your doing, wasn't it?'

'It was. Even in the wake of the first murder, Rintaro was bold enough to leave that photo of Hisako up in the darkroom, but I wanted to provide additional evidence for his motives and actions. I thought of the extra telephone after Sawako falsely claimed to have seen her father in the phone booth. I decided to hide it in the closet in the attic just in case. If I'd had time, I'd have found some excuse to get Akimitsu's shorthand note into Kenkichi's hands, so that it would make sense for his fingerprints to be on it. Of course, I failed to realize that the note Akimitsu handed me wasn't the original I'd written. If I'd found an opportunity to hand it to Kenkichi, there would have been no need to burn it and create a replacement. Still, the extra telephone provided crucial evidence for the idea that Rintaro had produced the transcript while listening in on the call.'

'Indeed. But Sawako knew what you were up to. She'd seen Kenkichi making the phone call to the hotel and realized what you two were planning. She loved you so much that she not only covered for you with her false testimony but was willing to take her own life to stop the truth from coming to light. Tell me, when you realized she'd discovered your secret, what prevented you from simply bumping her off like the others?'

'I was never out for blood, Mr Ishikari. Sawako played no role in the first part of the tragedy. If she *had* cracked and confessed the truth to the police, I'd have given myself up willingly. I'd have considered it a sign that my revenge was not something the gods could allow.'

'Very noble of you. Still, in the end, she felt compelled to take her own life. True tragedy arises not from the demise of the guilty or morally feeble, but from the suffering of the righteous, the innocent, the resolute. Once the curtain has lifted on the stage, there's no stopping the drama from unfolding. Who knows—perhaps Sawako's tragic end was inevitable from the moment she was born out of wedlock.

'There's one more thing I want to ask you. How did you persuade Kenkichi to act as your accomplice?'

'Mr Ishikari, the answer to that question lies, in a sense, in the misguided educational policy of the war period. For all those years, we drummed into the nation's children a pointless hatred of the enemy, a misguided desire for revenge. Children's hearts aren't like those of adults; the emotions seared into them cannot simply be forgotten overnight. Perhaps an extended period of democratic education will one day succeed in reversing the harm that was done. Otherwise, this country will be doomed to repeat the tragedies of its past.

'Kenkichi was a sensitive and precocious child. He knew that his sister had been subjected to a humiliation that beggared description. Any child his age is already susceptible to a vague pessimism about the world; on top of that, he had probably begun to sense that his days were numbered. And then I came back from the war and showed him some of the letters his sister had sent me. After seeing them, together with various other pieces of evidence, Kenkichi came to me of his own accord, saying he wanted revenge.

'But this wasn't something to be undertaken lightly; I needed to know I could rely on him. Mr Ishikari, do you remember when we walked past this house and saw the masked figure in the window? That was Kenkichi; I put him up to it as a way of proving his commitment, while simultaneously drawing your attention to the Chizui mansion and strengthening my position in that regard. It also helped put Taijiro on edge. The phone calls to the undertaker and the Oka Asylum, which Kenkichi also made at my request, served a similar purpose.

'The poor boy kept his promise to the very end. When Rintaro cornered him and threatened him, he pretended he'd go along with his cousin's plan—only to thwart it at the final moment. Even his decision to take poison makes a certain kind of sense. That's right, Mr Ishikari. Rintaro was never the type to get his hands dirty like that. By cutting short his own brief life, Kenkichi knew he'd be able to keep his pledge to me and deal Rintaro a final, fatal blow.'

'To ensure the success of your revenge, Kenkichi offered himself up as yet another victim ... The tragedy of this family really knows no bounds. Koichi, I have all the information I need. But tell me, what was the purpose of that spray of maple leaves and the snake-scale Noh costume?'

'That line you kept repeating, about how the demon always carried a prop, had me completely stumped. In my desperation, I decided to leave those unrelated Noh props lying around in an attempt to confuse you.'

'Funny. The prop was that ice axe, and you were the one who'd used it—and yet you still didn't realize what I meant ...'
I slowly got to my feet.

'Mr Ishikari, aren't you going to arrest me?' asked Koichi, looking up at me in surprise.

'As I said, I came here today as a regular citizen—as Hiroyuki Ishikari. And regular citizens don't have the right to arrest people. For your sake, just this once, I have defied the law. Now, that's hardly fitting behaviour for a prosecutor. As such, I intend to remove myself from public duty. I will hand in my resignation tomorrow.

'The perpetrator of the Chizui family murders will be officially recorded as Rintaro Chizui. The truth will remain between you, me, Mr Takagi and the gods. Your punishment is for you alone to decide. I know you, Koichi; you wouldn't have taken the lives of three people if you weren't ready to face the consequences. As your fellow human, and not as a prosecutor, I urge you to do what is necessary. I'm sure Mr Takagi will understand. Indeed, he may be the only one left to cry and offer flowers at your grave ...'

'Thank you, Mr Ishikari. I'm more grateful than I can say. At the same time, I think I understand how you must feel about all of this, too. And there is one other person who will be weeping for you, even if it is from beyond the grave.'

'You mean Kenkichi?'

'No, not him. Mr Ishikari, when Kayoko was at death's door, I leaned in closer than anyone else. I heard her say something that no one else seemed to catch. The words she uttered—her last in this world—were these: *Kayoko Ishikari*. That was her final parting gift.'

My heart was racing; tears began to trickle down my face. Through them, I felt I could see a double rainbow, the third in my life ...

'Thank you, Koichi. Do you remember that double rainbow that brought you back into my life? Well, more than two decades ago, when Kayoko had not yet married Professor Chizui, and I fell in love with her here by the sea, we witnessed the very same marvel.

'If rainbows symbolize anything, surely it is love—our fragile dream of a heavenly kind of happiness, one that can never be realized here on earth … You and I have each pursued our own double rainbow over the Chizui household, haven't we? In the end, both our lives seem to have been nothing more than a hunt for that elusive mirage …'

*

I had been standing on the shore for quite some time. With those final words from Kayoko, the one incessant regret that had plagued me for the past two decades or more—half my lifetime, in fact—had finally eased. As the gloom of evening deepened around me, I felt her warm breath on my face once again. I heard a voice singing in the distance, and soon the voice became hers, whispering in my ears: *My dear Hiroyuki, you waited for me all this time. Now, I'm finally free. I'll never leave you again. The two of us are bonded for eternity …*

I paced along the shore in vague pursuit of the voice. Neither the sparkle of the noctilucas as they scattered on the crests of the waves, nor the chorus of insects in the grass, nor even the glittering constellations of fireworks on the other side of Tokyo Bay were able to hold my attention. For the longest time, I simply wandered along the shore, seeking something I knew I could never obtain.

Before I knew it, it was past midnight. Every so often, the blood-red half-moon would emerge from behind the leaden clouds, bathing the shore in its impossibly bright light. A strong wind was blowing; the clouds drifted quickly overhead. In a narrow rift between them, a shooting star made its brief plummet towards the ocean. In the infinite stillness of that night, I thought I heard the murmuring of eternity.

Just then, the silence was broken by the clanging of a fire bell. I gathered myself and looked around. Red flames were rising from the promontory on which the Chizui mansion stood. As far as I knew, there were no other buildings in that area. Gripped by unease, I hurried back towards it.

At first I could only see the occasional flicker of flames amid a cloud of black smoke, but before long a terrifying pillar of fire had formed. The occasional flashes of purple and green must have been the chemicals in the laboratory exploding. The Chizui mansion was entirely enveloped in flames.

A sudden gust of wind whipped my hat from my head and into the vortex of fire. The flames were growing more frenzied by the minute.

Just then, I noticed one of the maids standing at my side. Her face was covered in soot, her hair tangled and messy. With bloodshot eyes she gazed vacantly into the blaze. More than anything else, I found myself staring at the traces of blood on her hands.

'What happened?'

'Miss Hisako got in an awful bad way all of a sudden. She passed away just now. I was so exhausted afterwards that I fell asleep, and when I woke up …'

Immediately grasping what had happened, I began walking towards the mansion.

By now I could feel the fire's heat on my face. I was searching for something amid the conflagration.

Then, amid the red flames engulfing one of the upstairs windows, I saw a figure.

'Koichi!'

Perhaps he heard my cry; in any case, the figure turned and seemed to wave a final farewell. At that very instant, the fire burst right through the roof and spread its great red wings into the sky. The very frame of the mansion began collapsing in front of my eyes. A salty wind blew up from the sea below, sending sparks whirling high into the sky, while the red moon, still visible through the column of thick black smoke, silently cast its light over what remained of the Chizui mansion.

Firelight, moonlight—I let them both wash over me. And, in the twin roar of the wind and the blaze, I heard, once again, the whisper of eternity.

13

The Sealed Note From Hiroyuki Ishikari

Mr Takagi, together with Koichi's journal and my letter, I am also sending you this confession. By now you should be familiar with almost the entire truth of the Chizui family tragedy. I am confident you will fully understand the decision I took—not as a prosecutor, but as a friend—with regard to Koichi's fate.

I have now retired from my position; I write to you merely as a civilian. Indeed, having at long last brought the Chizui tragedy to its conclusion, I have one final duty to carry out in this life.

Before I departed from the Chizui mansion for the last time, Koichi murmured the following to me: 'Mr Ishikari, I just can't get my head around the idea that Rintaro would commit suicide. And yet *I* certainly didn't poison him. What I wanted, more than anything, was for him to suffer. Sending him so instantly and painlessly to the other world was never part of my plan.'

'Koichi,' I replied, 'I am as convinced as you are that he was not the type to commit suicide. But this life, and with it the human heart, contain depths we will never fathom. Let us try to forget what happened. Faced with the incomprehensible, all we can do is accept it as the truth.'

Mr Takagi, I'm sure you, too, found it hard to believe that Rintaro committed suicide. To tell the truth, I didn't believe it either. In fact, I knew someone else had killed him—because that someone was me.

You see, I was convinced we'd never be able to bring Rintaro before a court. Even supposing we did, his sentence would, in all likelihood, be infinitely lighter than his heinous crimes deserved. When it came to this part of his plan, Koichi had miscalculated. And so I made up my mind. I would act not as a prosecutor, but as a human. I, not Koichi, would take Rintaro's life, and in doing so establish him, beyond any doubt, as the perpetrator of these murders. The diabolical fate he had concocted for my first and only love, Kayoko, had steeled my heart.

On the day of the final confrontation, I lingered in the laboratory after Koichi had left and slipped a dose of cyanide into my pocket. I gave Yoshino and Koichi tasks to attend to, thereby ensuring I was the first person in the dining room. I had the maids bring some tea. There was more than enough time to dissolve the cyanide in Rintaro's cup.

Mr Takagi, I am surprised by how at peace I am with my actions. The fact is I don't feel an inkling of remorse for what I did. Still, one thing is certain: I have broken the law. Koichi broke the law too, and look how severely I judged him. It would be beyond hypocritical of me to be lenient on myself where I have always been so strict on others. My work in this world is done. By the time this letter and its accompanying documents reach you, I will have departed on a journey from which there is no return. I have already decided on my final resting place. I ask only that you do nothing to disturb me from where I lie.

The Chizui family grave is at a temple just outside Tsuruki in Ishikawa prefecture. It is a rather picturesque spot, on the banks of the Mikawa river. But it is on the snowy slopes of nearby Mount Hakusan, where no one will ever visit, that I intend to end my days.

When the winter ends, the snow that has enveloped me will thaw in the glorious spring sun, and the Mikawa river will carry me to Kayoko's final resting place.

A love like melting snow; our only witness the budding willows. With every advent of spring, until the end of time, we shall be reunited.

Farewell, Mr Takagi. It is with gladness that I depart from this world. And, with my death, I hope to finally lower the curtain on this—the terrible tragedy of the Chizui family.

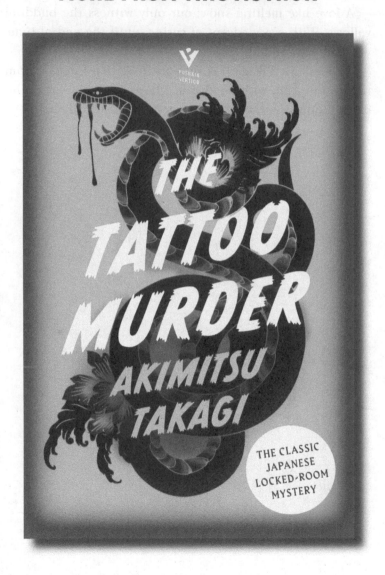